PRAISE FOR

Robert Stone AND *Fun with Problems*

"In the long form or the short, American fiction has no greater master than Robert Stone. These stories burn with his dark and incandescent magic."

—Madison Smartt Bell, author of *Devil's Dream*

"Once again, Stone displays his tense mastery of narrative, inexplicably fine dialogue, and what is perhaps the most sublime sense of any living writer for beginnings and endings. He is, simply, one of our best."

—Tom Bissell, author of *The Father of All Things*

"[Stone] pays his reader the deep compliment of refusing to simplify his creations. They are as flawed and sophisticated and complex and conflicted and naughty and tempted and contradictory and brutal and surprising as readers themselves . . . *Fun with Problems* is a book for grownups, for people prepared to absorb the news of the world that it announces, for people both grateful and a little uneasy in finding a writer brave enough to be the bearer."

—*New York Times Book Review*

"Stark and beautiful . . . it's impossible not to be impressed by Stone's audacity, steel-eyed honesty, and cold and sometimes bizarre sense of humor . . . an enlightening [read] and hard to forget . . . [Stone is] an American master."

—*National Public Radio*

Fun with Problems

Fun *with* Problems

STORIES

Robert Stone

MARINER BOOKS

HOUGHTON MIFFLIN HARCOURT

BOSTON   NEW YORK

For Jane and Emily

First Mariner Books edition 2010
Copyright © 2010 by Robert Stone

ALL RIGHTS RESERVED

For information about permission to reproduce selections from this book,
write to Permissions, Houghton Mifflin Harcourt Publishing Company,
215 Park Avenue South, New York, New York 10003.

www.houghtonmifflinbooks.com

Library of Congress Cataloging-in-Publication Data
Stone, Robert, date.
Fun with problems : stories / Robert Stone.
p. cm.
ISBN 978-0-618-38625-3
I. Title.
PS3569.T6418F86 2010
813'.54—dc22   2009013748
ISBN 978-0-547-39453-4 (pbk.)

Book design by Brian Moore

Printed in the United States of America

DOC 10 9 8 7 6 5 4 3 2 1

The following stories in this collection originally appeared elsewhere: *The
New Yorker*: "Fun with Problems." *Playboy*: "Honeymoon," "Charm City,"
"The Archer." *Open City*: "High Wire."

Overcoming difficulties can present spiritual opportunities.
It is actually possible to have fun with problems.

— REHAB VIDEO, CALIFORNIA, 1999

Contents

Fun with Problems

....

HAMPTON COUNTY LOCKED them down in a nine-teenth-century brick fortress of a jail, a penitential fantasy of red brick keeps and crenellations. The sight of it had twisted many a cocky smile. Citizens waiting at its marble stoop could contemplate the solipsisms of razor wire and the verse of all-weather civic poetry on the rosy keystone: LEARN TO LABOR AND TO WAIT.

Most of the time, Peter Matthews, an aging attorney with the public defender's office, liked the place for its spooky melodrama. On the days his presence was required there, he had a six-mile country drive to town. In summer or fall, when the weather was nice, it could be very pleasant. The unimproved road followed a high wooded ridge that enfolded the oxbows of a wide, slow-moving river. Corn and shade tobacco grew along the banks, and two of the switch-backs had preserved wooden bridges. In ice or wintry weather, the drive was work.

One Monday, toward the end of the football season, Matthews took a call from a young Cape Cod burglar called Georgie Laplace. Laplace, who was heedless and unlucky, had involved himself in the theft and disposal of some turquoise Hopi jewelry. To clear their books, the police on the Cape had constructed a useful narrative around him. Then they had transported Georgie clear across the state to Hampton's monster jail, where, it was hoped, he would succumb to homesickness and fear and endorse their version in court.

It was an outrage. In spite of the weather, Matthews decided to drive in.

On television, they were advertising the game later that night with file footage from Miami. Matthews lingered at the tube just long enough to glimpse the sunny margin of the field and get a blimp's-eye view of the shoreline. Since his divorce, he had been renting two rooms in a former bed-and-breakfast, a big farmhouse secured from the road by an absentee farmer's cornfields. It was a quiet place, comfortable enough when his mood was right. His fellow tenants were a couple of retired New York schoolteachers who lived upstairs and a tall man named Stokely, a locksmith on salary from a local hardware store who drove the company car. Everyone got on well. Nodded greetings and agreeable observations were exchanged. The owners of the property, Mr. and Mrs. Esquivel, lived in another farmhouse, fifty yards off: they had fled Colombia in the grip of La Violencia and had little tolerance for conflict.

On his way to the carport, Matthews noticed Mrs. Esquivel's cold, experienced eye on him. Little escaped her.

He eased the car over the wet double track to the paved road and started on his way to town. The ride was faster and easier by interstate, but Matthews had his ritual commitment to the two-lane road. That wet afternoon, it gave him little pleasure. The horizon had closed around him, and he moved in the face of an icy rain that thickened on his windshield wipers. At the first stop sign, he skidded, ending up at a crazy angle to the yellow line. After that, he turned up the radio for company, but there were only call-ins. Whiners, know-it-alls, Christers. An alienated lot.

In the depths of his soul, Matthews hated Hampton County. The local press sometimes idealized the place as the Happy Valley. Matthews liked to amuse his friends by calling it the Unhappy Valley, and he had a repertory of cruel, funny anecdotes about it. At the same time, the Valley was a particularly easy jurisdiction in which to make a living. His ambitions had faded, and life could be various and perversely satisfying in Hampton. When Matthews launched into his Unhappy Valley routine it was his own life and fortunes he was describing, and most days he could tolerate those well enough.

In fact, the Valley was his native place, and he had been watching it all his life: its preachifying and its secret horrors. The recently arrived professionals, academics and technologists, had brought to Hampton a self-conscious blessed assurance, unaware of the beatings, arson and murder that thrived in the hills around their white-trim shutters. Matthews knew the place's black heart. It was his living. Where the road descended to the river, a mile short of the first covered bridge, there stood a lone wooden tenement, the survivor of a company street of mill houses dating from the in-

dustrial age. All its companion houses had burned to the
ground years before. Nearly every time Matthews passed
the house, he saw children, a squadron of little whitey tow-
heads who, in the time he had lived at the Esquivels', seemed
never to change in age or approximate numbers. The house
was unpainted and usually had one of its windows glazed in
plastic.

Through the sleet, he saw one of the children standing
in an open doorway, dressed for a summer afternoon. It was
a girl of about ten, in baggy jeans and a yellowing, ragged
hand-me-down T-shirt. She stood absolutely still, indifferent to the stings of the weather, unblinking. She wore a
necklace of glass stones and shiny metal. Her stare was pro-
found and uneasy-making.

He waved to her, and she was gone. When he pulled out
to cross the intersection, it was as though she had not been
there.

He thought perhaps the solitude was finally getting to
him, leaving him impulsive and eccentric, even on his sober days. Especially on his sober days, each one marked with
small errors of judgment. The sight of children sometimes
made him homesick for his married past, getting his son to
school, drinking a beer with his wife.

During the seventies, everyone had said it was a tough
time to bring up children; in fact, it went on being that way.
The eighties and the nineties were no better. He and his
wife had been lucky. Their only boy was sensible and de-
cent, partaking of his mother's rectitude and perhaps a little
too much of his own "pessimism." So there was that at least.
He called the thing he had pessimism.

Halfway up a hillside, a turn-of-the-century Volvo passed

him with cheery disregard. Its bumper sticker read "We Are One Family," the town motto — the reference was to the imagined relationship between Hampton's inhabitants and those of the great globe itself, which was displayed in congenial artsy abstract, a smiley-face Planet Earth complete with latitudes and longitudes. Was it more frightening to raise children in the place Hampton had become? He could hardly say; his perspective was that of a criminal lawyer who knew the annals of wickedness.

A couple of miles farther on, Matthews came in sight of town. The famous jail, the red brick rat-house minarets attached to a new wing of frosted Martian glass, stood beside the river between a pair of old paper mills, whose lofts were now mainly occupied by artists in flight from the city. There were also a few shabby offices, headquarters to some social-services organizations. These were relics of the age of concern, grown decadent with underfunding, long on ideology and short on practical solutions. One scarred band specialized in raiding the migrant-pickers' cockfights. A crazy poet did children's theater the children dreaded.

Matthews parked his car in the sheriff's lot and eased up the marble steps to the old entrance. In a worn canvas case he had the recorded life and works of George Edgar Laplace. Settled in the lawyers' area, Matthews checked his records. At his previous arrest, the kid had been still too young for Hampton; the conditions of his sentencing specified some form of juvenile detention. This time they could keep him there.

As a child, George had been incorrectly diagnosed as retarded and spent years in the State School, equipped with all too much of the self-awareness he was supposed to have been spared. Some of the more dedicated teachers there had befriended him. But the school was run not by its staff but by inmate youths of perfectly adequate intelligence, eccentric only in their cruelty and unwanted at home. George inclined to drugs for self-medication. The drugs placed him in a criminal milieu, a quarter badly suited for such an unadventurous, asthmatic, overimaginative person.

Of course, Matthews thought, the system required Georgies. It might be that justice itself required Georgies.

He became a punk, a snitch, a white rat, the man never to be used honorably, since he respected only the threat of violence, who could, for the good vainly done him, return only treachery. Fear was his only friend and master. The wise hard-hearted English politician had correctly foretold Georgie Laplace — his soul was a slave's.

Poor Georgie, thought Matthews, fishing through the young man's paper. The guy's worst affliction was his sharp comprehension. He scudded around the state's jail system with his intelligence soldered to his back like a bottle rocket pinned by a State School sadist to a frog. He even had the wit not to ask why. It made him interesting company. It made him worth fighting for sometimes.

Matthews and his client conferred in a chapel in the jail's old wing, a relic of gentler days. The chapel had been temporarily divided by partitions of wallboard and Plexiglas that reached a third of the way to the ceiling and were being slowly vandalized.

There were a couple of conferences in progress that afternoon, and quarters were close. The two guards, whom the inmates called "hacks," could hear every conversation from their station. Matthews's young client, across the misted plastic and dirty wallboard, looked frightened out of his wits.

Thirty-five feet away, at another partition, a maniac called Brand was in what looked like flirtatious conversation with a tall toothy red-headed woman. It was of Brand that Georgie Laplace was particularly frightened.

"He's gonna break my fingers, man," Georgie told his lawyer. "He said that. He told me he was gonna break my fingers at lunch."

Georgie's half-whispered, stuttering terror was distracting to Matthews, who was trying to extract Georgie's particulars from a welter of false and misleading documents.

Matthews put his glasses on to look at Brand, a kind of local character, though quite a dangerous one. Matthews had seen him before: a man about thirty, powerfully built. He had curly blond hair that cascaded over his brows with cavalier deviltry. In spite of his silly fair mustache, girls, often to their subsequent regret, found him wicked cute.

Brand, without question, was destined for the hospital. The word on the block was that to get into the hospital you had to do something queer enough to make the tabloids. If you pulled weird shit, maimed some fuck, you might get hospital time. Matthews was also taken with the man's visitor, who seemed to represent the educated classes.

"Brand's gonna break my fingers, no shit," Georgie was saying.

Brand's visitor had laid out a set of tarot cards on the surface provided on her side of the barrier. She seemed to be charting her patient's destiny.

"Did he tell you he'd break your fingers?" Matthews asked.

"Fuckin'-A right he told me! He says, 'What you bet I can break your fingers? Not everybody could do it,' he says. 'Most wouldn't do it,' he says."

"So what did you say to that?" Matthews asked.

"What did I say? What would you say?"

"Keep your voice down," Matthews said.

The young woman sat very tall. She wore an ankle-length suede skirt and boots and a turtleneck top that favored, in Matthews's view, the swell of her small breasts and firm shoulders.

Matthews watched them. The woman was laughing at something Brand had said, and Matthews felt a rush of what he thought might be a very basic form of sexual jealousy. Here, safely confined, we had self-selected alpha man, recognizable by his readiness to snap off your digits on a whim, exchanging a few sexual signifiers with the condescending female of the species. It wasn't pretty, but it was the real thing.

"Hey, counselor," Georgie wailed. Instinctively, he lowered his voice. "How about gettin' me out of this tank?"

"Lay low for a while," Matthews whispered. They both watched Brand. "You know how it's done. Hey, who's the broad with him? Not his wife?"

Georgie almost smiled. "She's a shrink, man. She's his shrink."

"With tarot cards?"

"She's, like, telling his fortune," Georgie explained.

"Okay," Matthews told him. "Just stay away from him. Try not to attract his attention."

"Oh, yeah," Georgie said. "Good fuckin' luck."

"I'll have a word with the administration tomorrow. We'll get you moved. Trust me."

Georgie's face fell. "Tomorrow? I thought today. You got my hopes up."

"You're too much of an optimist. Some things can't be done in a day. Make it through the night," Matthews said. "You'll be okay tomorrow."

Matthews watched his client walk out of the chapel. And sure enough, the man called Brand, ignoring his pretty adviser, turned predatory eyes on Georgie Laplace.

The prison-rights people called the place a "zoo," but it was worse, Matthews thought; it was a fish tank, a vivarium. The men in it had been reduced beyond apes; they were devolving into the stuff under the pine needles on the forest floor. Some of them bit. The big ones ate the little ones.

So Matthews had to picture Brand and Laplace back there in the supposedly secure new wing. *Jeopardy!* on the box, Georgie Laplace sitting on his hands, ignoring his baloney sandwich, watching for his enemy. On one side, Brand, precognitive superman; on the other, Georgie Laplace, Baconian villain.

Matthews stuffed his papers in the case and started out. He felt depressed and edgy; angry, too. It was the wretched, dangerous time of day, and he was all the things the program said you should not be. Hungry. Angry. Alone.

The pretty counselor still had her tarot cards spread out on the surface of the barrier. She called after her client.

"Don't forget to take your meds, Mr. Brand."

Brand turned and laughed at her, possessor of a beautiful secret. Matthews shuddered. He stopped in the chapel doorway for a moment and felt something move against his foot. One of the jailhouse cats, a huge gray eunuch, wrapping itself against his calf and ankle. Part Persian, with a fluffy neck and huge stupid eyes, the cat was a survivor of milder, homelier days at the jail. The old main section had looked like the Big House in a Cagney movie, but had been in fact a reasonable place where the sheriff and his family lived with their cats. There were no family accommodations now, and the surviving cats simply made trouble.

Matthews pulled his foot away.

"Beat it," he told the thing. On the whole, he liked cats. "Scram."

A broad-breasted, tough-looking, gray-haired woman came through the door and took the cat in her arms.

"Jackie," she said to it. "Hey, Jackie, watcha doin' in the chapel?" She was wearing a ski outfit and a New England Patriots watch cap. "Watcha doin', huh?"

A hack beside the chapel door said, "Hi, Sister."

"Hiya, Charlie." She stroked the cat under its chin and looked at Matthews. "Hiya, bub. Lawyer, are ya?"

"That's me," Matthews said.

The woman was called Sister Sophia. She was a nun or an ex-nun; Matthews had never got it quite clear. She functioned as a social worker, employed by one of the neighboring service agencies, and as the prison's Catholic chaplain.

For her part, she seemed a jolly soul. She had seen him many times before but seemed never to be able to distinguish one lawyer from another.

With the cat slung across her forearm, she looked over the chapel, where the young psychologist was carefully wrapping her tarot deck in a beige silk handkerchief.

"I see something I don't like," the nun said. She carried the cat out through an open metal door, released it into the office area and came back. "I see a lot of superstitious — I don't want to use the S-word!"

"Are you talking to me?" the red-headed therapist asked.

"Yeah. I'm talking to you," the nun said. "What do you think you're doing, missy? Think you're playing cosmic Monopoly there?"

"Do you mean my Tarot Oracle?" the psychologist asked.

"That's right. I don't go for that kind of stuff."

"It's a therapeutic device," the young woman said. "The cards help them to talk about themselves." She turned for support to Matthews, who had been observing her. "It relaxes them."

Matthews thought her voice sounded local; her background was probably fairly humble, otherwise her family would have invested in some improving orthodontics for such a basically pretty girl.

"Maybe she's got something there," he told Sister Sophia, although he saw little point in making Brand crazier than he already was.

The lippy nun looked at Matthews for a moment and turned back to the psychologist.

"That stuff is diabolical superstition," she declared. "It stands between the soul and Higher Power." The gray cat came back through the metal door to listen like a familiar. Unchallenged, the nun grew triumphalist. "Ha! Here she is," she said, nodding toward the psychologist, "supposed to be helping these kids!" She looked up and down the visiting area as though in search of a larger audience. "Tarot cards!" she cried. "Phooey!"

An elderly prisoner with a push broom came out behind the cat.

"We're fucking entitled," the old man said.

"You just watch your language, Bobby," a passing guard told him.

The young woman blushed. "They *are* entitled," she said. "They're entitled to any kind of therapy. And it does not interfere with Higher Power. Insight promotes it." The psychologist was pointing at the crucifix that still stood on the edge of the altar at the near end of the room. "What if I say that's superstition?" Addressing Matthews now, she startled the cat. "I bet it's unconstitutional. I mean, where's the wall of separation?"

"Well," Sister said, outraged and gesturing at the psychologist's cards, "I better not find any of these magic doozies around the plant, because I'll get 'em lifted."

"I'm sure you can do that, Sister," the red-headed psychologist said. "You serve the county instead of the inmates. You're a snitch."

Everyone was horrified.

"Did you hear her?" Sister Sophia asked the men. "Did you hear what she called me?"

In fact, it was generally believed that Sister Sophia —

though a good enough egg in her own way — had her own interpretations of the unwritten laws. And that there were certain things better left uncommitted to her discretion.

"Maybe you should apologize to Sister Sophia," the hack said. "Ya went too far there."

"Heat of argument," Matthews said.

Sister Sophia gathered up the cat and fixed them each in turn with a dreadful wounded stare. She was a person completely of the jail, and the accusation was a mortal one. Matthews wondered how well the psychologist understood this. She seemed not to have been around for very long.

Lights flashed. The amplified voice of the administration declared visitations concluded. The hack urged them out.

"Let's go home, folks."

Sister Sophia and Jackie, padding underfoot, retreated up the stone passageway.

"After thirty years!" Sister Sophia said, following the big neutered tom up the dank stone hallway. "Thirty years in this crummy joint!"

"Just a misunderstanding," Matthews said to the young woman. He extended a hand. "Pete Matthews." Her name was Amy Littlefield.

They lingered in the severe dark-wood reception room.

"You know," Matthews said, "your guy is threatening my client."

"Oh," she said. "He's always boasting. He told me the test of a tough guy was to break someone's fingers." A guilty smile appeared on her face and faded immediately. "He's trying in his way to impress me."

On Water Street, outside the jail, it was cold and cheerless. Fine hail rattled against the streetlights and the steps of the jail.

"Impressed?"

"He needs to take his antipsychotics. He doesn't belong in there. I mean," she said, "what can you do?"

"I was wondering that. I'm worried about Georgie."

"Really? Your client looks tough."

"No," Matthews explained. "No. The last time he was in there," Matthews said, "he was underage. I got him out on habeas corpus. Now he thinks I'm a miracle worker."

"Good luck," she said.

They parted ways in the gathering sleet. Matthews took the river sidewalk with his shoulder to the force of the storm off the river. He followed the embankment to the edge of the downtown mill buildings. Then he suddenly turned back and went in the direction that Amy had gone. When she heard him coming up behind her, she stopped and moved back from the sidewalk.

"What did you mean," Matthews asked, "he doesn't belong in there?"

She laughed. "What did I mean? I meant he was crazy. He should be in a hospital."

"Right."

"Did you think I was taking his side? That I thought he was a nice guy?"

"I wasn't sure. You're a social worker."

She shook her head.

He looked up and down the street and she watched. He thought she was about to ask him if he was looking for something.

"So, Amy," he said, "would you like a drink?"

She laughed in a strangely embarrassed way. The quality of her embarrassment was somehow familiar to him.

"I don't drink," she said gaily. As though the statement did not necessarily foreclose sociability.

"Well," he said, "have an *Apfel-schorle!*"

"I don't know what that is."

"You've fallen into the right hands," Matthews said. The young psychologist stopped in her tracks. She shielded the lenses of her glasses from the icy rain with one hand and pulled her plaid scarf over her bright hair. Little hailstones clung to the russet strands like coral clusters, not melting.

"Wait a minute," she said. "I haven't fallen into your hands."

"No," Matthews said. "Of course not." He was wondering whether she thought him too old for her. She did not seem much over thirty-five.

"Oh," she said. There was another slightly embarrassed laugh. Like the first, it made him hopeful.

"I'm not surprised you're a psychologist, Amy."

"Really?" she asked, as they hurried out of the weather. "Why?"

He had only been mocking her. Matthews's life had become so solitary he had almost stopped caring what he said, or to whom.

They went to the restaurant where, sober, Matthews had discovered *Apfel-schorle*, mixed apple juice and soda. The place was run by a German hippie who cooked and his

American graduate-student wife. Its ambience was not at all gemütlich, but gray-black Euro-slick. The waitress was a stylish, somber German exchange student.

"Funny," Amy said when they had ordered a *schorle* for her and a Scotch for Matthews, "that they'd still serve such a summer drink in the winter."

Matthews agreed that it was funny.

"Aren't you hungry?" he asked her.

She cast the question off with her peculiar gaiety. Matthews tried to inspect her further without being spotted. Her red hair seemed natural: she had the right watery-blue eyes and freckled skin. In her strong lean face, the long-lashed, achromatic eyes looked wonderfully dramatic. Effects combined to make her seem sensitive, innocent and touchingly plain. Vulnerable.

Across the table, he indulged in some brief speculation about her character and inner life. Her facing down fatuous Sister Sophia was admirable in a way, but it was also self-righteous and overwrought. Pretty ruthless, really, calling the poor woman a snitch. And Amy herself seemed not much smarter than the nun, all fiery bread and roses, the blushing champion of free thought with her fucking wall of separation.

In fact, at that moment Matthews did not want to care what Amy was like. His life was lonely enough, but he was not shopping for a friend or a comrade in the service of the poor. His attraction to her was sensual, sexual and mean, which was how he wanted it. Spite had taught him detachment. The trick was to carry on indifferent to his own feelings and without pity for things like Amy's ditsy vagueness or the neediness she was beginning to display.

"Sure you won't have something stronger?"

She shook her head. Now, he observed, she was all reticence and demurrals — no drink, no dinner, no nothing. Yet, on a certain level, he thought, she acted like someone who wanted to play.

"I liked your standing up to Sister Sophia," Matthews told her when he had his second drink in hand.

She did not seem entirely pleased by his compliment. For a few seconds, she only looked at him without speaking.

"I felt kind of sorry afterward. I shouldn't have called her a snitch."

"I wouldn't worry about it. She's a bully." He watched her fidget unhappily on her big wooden chair. To make any progress it would be necessary to cheer her up. Win her over. "And she really is a snitch."

"Oh, God," said Amy. "That makes it worse."

"Yes, it does," Matthews said. He laughed at her in spite of himself. "Sorry."

"So," she said, "I was being stupid."

"No, no. I admired what you did." He felt a little ashamed of the contrived flattery. He had underestimated her.

"I was being pompous pious."

"You were fine," he said. "I don't think you did anything inappropriate."

"Inappropriate" had become such a useful word, he thought, so redolent of the spirit of the times. Everyone had dumb, disastrous moments and behaved inappropriately. Inappropriate anger led to attacks of bad judgment. Misplaced idealism was also inappropriate. And almost everyone had a little no matter how clean they were.

"Really?" she asked.

"Really," he told her. "Have a drink." Somehow the suggestion turned her around this time. Her state of agitated regret seemed to visibly depart. The look he saw in her pale eyes was suddenly challenging and flirtatious.

"No, I don't think so," she said firmly. The firmness had a pretended note.

The mournful fräulein desired them to stop fiddle-fucking, order dinner or go away. Matthews set her pouting with another drinks order. *Apfel-schorle* for the little lady, another Scotch for himself. Amy went to the Ladies.

When the drinks came, Matthews was reminded of the celebrations at a wedding he had attended the previous weekend. Someone had proposed the toast *"l'chaim"* — "to life." There and then Matthews had decided it was a toast he would never, ever, willingly drink again. Not, of course, that he would make a scene about it. Returned, Amy thoughtfully considered her glass of juice.

"I've quit drinking for a while," she announced. Matthews thought she might be getting admirable again. In fact, he realized, she was offering him a wedge. How much might he pry?

"I think you should make an exception this evening. Really," he said. "You've been fighting the good fight." The words were ill chosen, he knew that. It was hard to stop making fun of her. The devil drove him. He labored to recoup. "I mean, you want to forget all that, right?"

"Well," she said, in the manner of one about to explain thoroughly, "see, I've been doing a play."

"A play?"

Amy told him about her second career. "I went to New

York for a year," she said. "I did some off-off-Broadway. I almost got Shakespeare in the Park."

"No kidding?"

"No kidding. It would have been fun."

"Shakespeare in the Park? Sounds like fun."

"But it was almost, right? No cigar."

A different Amy. Animation. Still, though, tinged with regret. "Anyway," Amy said, "I did some great stuff. Odets. Do you know Clifford Odets?"

"Sure. *Waiting for Lefty.*"

"We didn't do that. We did two minor short plays. And we did a dramatic reading of *John Brown's Body.*"

"Really? Who were you?"

"Don't tease me," she said. "Don't tease me about my year in New York."

"I wouldn't," Matthews said, because he had not been. "I think it's great."

"Well, not so great," she said, "because it's over and I have to make a living. And clinical psych is what I do."

"You do it very effectively."

"Yeah, sure," she said. It turned out she was not drinking because she thought alcohol interfered with remembering her lines. "I blank. I go up. You know, forget the cue and the line."

"I see."

"Drinking gives you these glitches," she said. For a moment, she put the tip of her tongue to her upper lip and looked around the place. There was one other occupied table. Two youngish faculty couples were finishing their chocolate cake. "I don't know, maybe it's just a superstition."

"I bet it is. What play are you doing?"

"*Cymbeline*. It's Shakespeare."

"I'm not very familiar with it."

"No, it's not often performed. It's kind of ridiculous on the level of plot. But it has its moments."

"Why don't you join me," Matthews said. "Have a drink. And we'll have something to eat."

"Do I have to?" she asked.

Afterward, he would have to ask himself why he had pressed her so hard. As though it were the senior prom and she were a high school virgin he wanted to addle with fruit wine. Asking him that way, she had seemed so gravely passive, supine, absurd. Asking for it. She would drink if he made her. So he did.

"Definitely."

"And what shall I drink?"

"What do you like?"

"I like margaritas," she said.

So they ordered her Teutonic margaritas, of which she consumed quite a few, straight up with salt, and a weight fell, finally, from her pretty shoulders. She told him about *Cymbeline*, which, on the level of plot, *did* sound ridiculous. They laughed about that. But when she professed to discover the other levels, they grew properly serious. She had plainly thought a lot about it, and about her character, named Imogen, an apparently ridiculous figure.

"And what's strange," she said, "is to come from rehearsal, to come from Shakespeare to the life of all these young community males in the jail."

For a moment, he did not know what she was talking

about. "Don't say things like 'young community males,'" he told her. "Don't use jargon."

She got huffy, blushed, and withdrew for a while. Ironic, because it was one thing said to her in friendship.

She lived in Hampton's old downtown, in what had been an office building but was now living space for a variety of the place's ambiguously connected people. "Nontraditional households" was how she would have put it.

"There's nothing to drink," she told him. "I don't keep it."

So they made a detour to the package store in the square to get Scotch, tequila and cheap margarita mix.

Her apartment had high ceilings and many windows adorned with plants. He thought that in the daytime it must have lots of light. On one wall there were theater posters and a few photographs of Amy in costume. He inspected them while, staggering ever so slightly, she went to change clothes.

In the kitchen, he worked loose her ice trays and made sloppy, overboozy drinks. She came back in gray-green tights with a sort of short, hooded burnous a shade lighter. Her glasses had lightly tinted lenses; she had let her hair down. They sat one cushion apart on an outsized brown leather sofa that looked as though it had come from some dean's office at the local college.

Settled on the sofa, she did a little snug wiggle.

"Oh, I like leather." She leaned her head back happily, then turned to him. "But it makes you sweat."

That should have been the moment, but he was distracted

by drink. He got anecdotal, told some favorite jailhouse horror stories at which they could laugh comradely progressive
laughter. Not too many. The subject was too depressing,
and he did not want to spoil things. Amy began to tell stories about some other place, a place she did not identify. A
hospital? He paid closer attention.

"So there was a woman at this place where I was."

"What place?"

"A woman at this place," Amy went on, "but it wasn't a
woman at this place."

"No?"

"No," Amy said. "It was me. It was" — she corrected herself with a humorous theatrical flourish. "It was I. It was a
spa, right? A really expensive health spa. Ever been to one?"
she asked him.

"Yes. Once."

She laughed at him, in the bag, unstoppable.

"I'm not talking about a drunk farm. Although I've been
to those too, I have to tell you."

"I have to tell you," he said, "I have too."

"But this," Amy said, "the setting of our story, was a very
fancy desert health spa." She stopped and looked at him as if
making sure she was among friends. Matthews did his best.
"I was going to tell this as somebody else's story. But it
was me."

"I see."

"Well," Amy said, "at this really expensive health spa
there was a clairvoyant? The clairvoyant picked me. Me,
right? He read my thoughts — that was the number."

His instinct was to stop her. A lawyerly impulse. A human
one? He didn't.

"And the clairvoyant revealed to me, and to everybody in the fancy spa, around the beautiful fire in the evening, the clairvoyant revealed to me that there were two men in my life. And that was right. It was God's truth. I had a husband who was not a very nice man. And I had a lover who, it turned out, was not so absolutely great either. As it turned out."

Her free hand, the one not holding the drink, began to tremble a little. As much as he wanted to, Matthews did not put out his own hand to steady it.

"So, when I went home, the spa gave me a record of my session with the clairvoyant. A recording — a tape, a CD, I don't know. And would you believe I forgot all about it? I forgot it utterly. Until —"

It was Amy's guessing game. She teased, grinning, tears beginning.

"Until your old man found it," Matthews said.

She pointed her index finger, bingo, at him.

"Until he found it. The prick. Excuse me. Until he found it. Whereupon he divorced me."

"I see."

"And in fact I began to drink. And in fact I later went to . . . the other sort of place you mean." She looked closely at him again. "I might have known you there."

"Yes, you might," he said, "but actually no."

"By then, my friend —" She stopped herself. "Ah, we're talking me, aren't we? Not my made-up friend."

"We're talking first-person."

"After the divorce, I needed a hospital, not a health spa. Get it?"

"Yes," he said. "I understand. I've been there."

"Of course," she said, "you've been there."

"Twice," Matthews said. "For varying lengths of stay."

"You and me," Amy said. "It might even have been the same place."

"That it might."

Amy stood up and leaned on the arm of her leather sofa.

"Drinking makes me want to smoke," she said. He looked up at her; leaning, she had cocked a hip in a kind of Attic stance, lifting the hem of the top she wore, turned away from him, searching for all the cigarettes in the world to smoke at once. Turned away but, as it were, presenting.

He put it all together very quickly, an instinct for the logic of events. The presenting stance, the abasement.

So he stood silently beside her. How easily he might have kissed her and held her. The impulse was there. He drew his hand back and whacked her, as hard as she might reasonably require.

The hit stunned her. She put a hand to her bottom, flushing nicely and trembling very slightly with the sting of it. Then they stood in the moment, on the brink of it. Poised between what? Absurdity and death, eros and thanatos, the screech of lust and Cymbeline? What the boys in the jail called "down-low shit."

But she did not call him vulgar names or question his sanity or turn in anger and astonishment. She said quietly, "I guess I deserved that."

"I guess you did," Matthews told her. His voice was stern and cold, though he took her by the hand. So they went to bed and there was some down-low shit. Had he not been distracted by his pleasure, Matthews would have congratulated himself on the soundness of his observations and his quick reaction time.

He was drunk but so inflamed there was no question of his flunking it. He let her guide him to what she liked; experience told him this was best. You let her guide you to what she liked and sometimes what she liked was a drag but often what she liked was delightful, an unsuspected turn, a novelty, warm and silky if not always very clean. So it was with Amy. Absolutely no rougher than she wanted it, he thought. Long-lasting and thorough.

All of that, but in the morning, when he came back from the bathroom, she was quietly crying. He had forced her to drink. Why had he done it? Well. He leaned his arm against the lintel of the bedroom door and rested his forehead on it in a posture like grief. Some remorse. Too bad.

After he had dressed in silence, he stood by her bed. Certainly he would have liked to reach out. Really, to reach out, to say, "I've been there, Amy, love. See how like you I am?" To lay a hand softly on the shoulder of which he had become fond. But she stayed where she was, and he went and left her alone with the first day of the rest of her life. Easy does it. Walking out to tears. So dispiriting.

He wrote his brief in sobriety the next day and called the deputy master of the jail about his client and Brand.

"The guy's dangerous. I was talking to his shrink."

"Tell me about it," said the deputy master.

He did all the things that duty required, but his first drink came not very late in the day. Happy hour at the Chinese restaurant in the strip mall that observed it early. Not-so-happy hour with the same Scotch he had been drinking. So anyone could see him take the same cup that late last night had killed his love. Atonement, the least he could do.

He did not call her that day or the next. But he did attend a performance of *Cymbeline* at the Community Theater. *Cymbeline*'s plot seemed ridiculous on every level he could imagine and he found its serious side impenetrable. The point of the production seemed to be the costumes and sets, which were inspired by Celtic art; there had been an exhibition of ancient Celtic artifacts at the college. The actors' gowns were clasped by torques like daggers, the cloth inset with disks that made them shimmer handsomely. The show had gone in for aromatherapy, perfuming the stage to enhance the sort of altered state it was after.

Amy as Imogen looked tired and a little blowzy beneath her makeup. He sat a few rows from the stage so as to be able to see her. He felt ashamed of what had happened, and he had to keep reminding himself that she probably could not see him in the darkness. She did apparently forget her lines at several points and fell back on mock Shakespeare. It was hard to tell. But when it came time for Imogen to die or pretend to die or whatever fateful thing it was the disguised Imogen did, Amy was very convincing.

The play had a few lines that reached him, impressed him enough to occasion a trip to the library.

> 'Twas but a bolt of nothing, shot at nothing,
> Which the brain makes of fumes: our very eyes
> Are like our judgments blind.

How true.

It occurred to him that her flustered reaction to Sister

Sophia's prattle about higher powers should have clued him early on. It was the program speaking; the diction of addiction. Himself and Amy and Sister Sophia, all rummies together.

In a better world, he thought, he might have been her friend. They might well have found themselves together in the place she talked about. On those grim rehab days that passed between hard, clear black lines, they might have had some fun. They might have formed a kind of madhouse friendship. Maybe more than friendship.

And it was not even impossible for him to imagine them, out in the world, soldiering together toward sobriety's sparkling horizon. They would be serving humanity and their higher power. Holding each other upright in Hampton jail, talking about walls of separation and the Rights of Man. The rights of humankind, to be sure. Talking *Cymbeline*.

But as Sister Sophia might have put it, he was her lower power. How could it be otherwise? He was the man whose ex-wife had once said of him, "You don't care whether you even get laid, as long as you can make some woman unhappy." In that capacity he had the goodness not to call her.

He did see Amy once again before the winter was over.

It was a small place. She was in a bar, still on the sauce, in the company of a man somewhat older than herself. Naturally, Matthews recognized the boyfriend as a sadistic creep.

She did not seem to hold anything against Matthews. Of course they were both loaded. Amy and the Community Theater had agreed to forgive each other's limitations. She would be appearing again in the spring. Not Shakespeare this time. Chekhov.

He wished her well. Seeing her again provided him a rush

from a pump, a hit from the daily drip of regret and loss. It was time for a drink.

There was a toast for everything. It fell to him, buying the round, to propose it. Here's to a shot at nothing? Here's to love in all its infinite variety? Not life — he was not doing that one.

He touched her glass merrily and said, "Break a leg, Amy."

Honeymoon

....

HE WOKE to the trilling of an island bird in the traveler's palm outside their hotel room. The palm's out-
line shimmied in the morning sunlight against the
aqua curtain. He was lustful and erect. He reached over to
touch the young woman he had married.

Feeling his hand on her skin, she slid into his embrace.

"What is it?" she asked, laughing.

"It's me."

She laughed herself awake, leaned up on her elbow, her
head back, blinking in the new light. The filtered glow of
day gilded her fair, disordered hair. When she turned to
him, her eyes were clear, guileless, happy.

"Not you, dope. The bird."

"In these islands," he said, "they call it a divi-divi bird."

"Divi-divi?" she repeated, in burlesqued Caribbean.
"Divi-divi."

Then she bent to him. He could not stop marveling at the
velvet quality of her skin.

Later, from the bathroom, she called, "And what's the language?"

"Papiamento."

She came out naked and drew the curtain back.

"Oh my God, it's heaven. Heavenly," she turned to tell him, already pulling on her bathing suit. "I'm going to the pool."

And she was gone, disappeared like a fragrance in motion, young magic. In the sad afterglow of his pleasure, he called his ex-wife.

"I can't believe you're calling me," she said.

"I'm on my honeymoon."

"Well," she said, "this time you get one."

"I can't do it," he told her. "I'm lonely to the bottom of my soul. I can't cope."

She began to cry. To cry for him. He wept himself.

"Scotty," she said, "I tried. I hated it. One thing after another. I let you."

"I want to come home," he said.

"I let you," she said. "One goddamn thing after another. I hated you drinking that way. I hated everything, but I never questioned you because I thought, Shit, he loves me. But you didn't."

"I swear," he said. "I do."

"And you finally did it, hurrah for you. And I said to myself, 'He's gone, I'll die, what will I live for?'"

"I'll come home."

"What will I live for? He's gone. Oh, poor little me. But now I think I'll live, Tiger. Fucking right," she said. "You wanted to be gone? Get gone. Have a great honeymoon."

"I'll come home," he said. But she had put the receiver down.

On their way to the reef, the dive boat cutting through the sparkling water, they saw flying fish.

"It's heaven," she said, and licked her lips. She was afraid, he saw. It was her first reef dive; she had only just taken up diving.

He thought she had never looked more beautiful. Golden-haired, tall and brave. Frightened, doing it to prove herself to him.

"You talked about diving in your class," she said. "The first one I took. And I swore to myself — one day I'll go diving with him. Isn't that awful?"

Maybe, he thought, she worried that God would punish her for adultery. She had been raised Catholic. The dive-master at the tiller looked at them in turn and smiled.

She was trembling as they got into their wet suits and struggled with the equipment. Then he saw the little vial of tablets in her hand. Valium. You saw it at every dive site, the Valium pills awash in the scuppers, the unsightly tubes dropped on the coral heads. Couples — one dived and the other sneaked Valium.

"Give me that," he said softly. "You won't need that. I'll be with you."

"Oh, shit," she said, "you caught me."

Neither of them wanted the divemaster to hear. When he was suited up, he slipped the vial into a utility pocket.

The light of day, the first hour after dawn. Pure as creation, he thought. She took his hand. He kept hearing the other woman's voice, the one whose skin was no longer so smooth, though it had been, twenty-five years before. *You wanted to go. Be gone.*

Helping her climb into the gear, her back to him, he raised the vial to his lips and took in as many of the tablets as he could. When her tank was in place, they each took a swallow of fresh water. She held his hand while the dive-master explained the currents. The morning sun found diamonds in the dun, quartz-veined rock around the bay.

It was a wall dive, and the wall was sublime. Elkhorn and rose coral. There were clouds of damselfish, angels and tang. The brilliant sunshine dappled it all and descended in great columns of light to the blue-gray deep.

He followed one and moved into the uncolored world of fifteen fathoms. The weight of the air took him down the darkening wall. Slowly, deliberately, he took off his tank. It sank with him in a dream, a gala of bubbles. Beyond pain and shadow, her fair, desired, long-limbed form diminished against the sky.

Charm City

....

AT A RECITAL one autumn evening Frank Bower heard Mahler's *Song of the Earth*, performed by four young singers. The part that moved him most was the faux Chinese poetry that ended in the poet's rapture. Bower's enjoyment was shadowed by anxiety and some distant unremembered grief. He was transfixed by the singer, a young Korean woman who performed with closed eyes in the posture of a supplicant. "*Abschied*," she sang. Rapture in spite of all. The music caused him some emotional confusion.

At the close of the movement the singer held her pose as though she herself did not recognize that the song was over. Bower's gaze settled on a tall woman in a leather coat who appeared to be looking straight at him. Whatever it was she saw so preoccupied her that she did not trouble to applaud after the last movement. He thought she must be a friend of his wife's whom he might have met once and forgotten.

When he left the auditorium Bower wandered into the museum's restaurant, a pleasingly simple room all lines and light, done in the futuristic severity of twenty years before. It had one glass wall transparent to the autumnal garden. Outside there were ivy and pines and leaves on the barren earth. It was growing dark but he could make out the shape of a metal structure and hear the sound of falling water. Bower was a technical writer for a software systems company in Towson who had briefly taught classics at Hopkins. He was naturally discontented with his work as with other things.

At the cafeteria counter he bought a mini-bottle of cabernet along with cheese and slices of apple. He took a table by the window and sat until it cast him his own reflection. He loved music. Mahler's bittersweet notes echoed in his mind's ear, taking their own direction, producing unvoiced melodies. *Abschied.* It was a Thursday night and the museum was open until eight.

Finally the wine made him hungry. He put his glasses and jacket on and prepared to go. About to rise, he realized there was a woman standing over his table. She was handsome, long-faced. The phrase "terrible gray eyes," read somewhere, occurred to him. She was forty-five or so, tall and well built. She wore a leather jacket fragrant with the rich piquant smell of hide. It was the woman he had locked eyes with in the auditorium.

"What would you say," the woman asked, "if I proposed to buy you a drink?"

He stared. Surely he must know her. She was laughing at his astonishment.

"Don't strange women often offer to buy you drinks?"

She set down the tray she was holding and put wine and another glass before him.

"That's very kind of you," Bower said. "How can I say no?"

"I hope you won't. May I sit down?"

He rose from his chair to invite her. When she was seated across from him, he waited for her to speak. She looked comfortable there, sipping her own wine.

"But we know each other," Bower asked her, "don't we?"

"They say it's a small world."

He thought her smile ambiguous. Maybe a little complacent and remote. Friend or foe? He laughed to please her, though he was troubled and embarrassed.

"I'm sorry," he said. He was trying to make her sudden presence more amenable to reason. "I can't remember where we met. I'm still trying to place you."

"What if I don't place? What if I'm a complete stranger?"

It stopped him. She was not young or trying to appear so. She seemed cultivated, not at all vulgar. In the tweed skirt that decorously showed her figure and the dashing leather jacket, she aroused his dormant lust to capture. At the same time, he noticed she wore a wedding ring.

"Will you tell me your name?"

He experienced a certain vague caution. He thought she might have seen that in his eyes, because she laughed at him again. She took a business card from her smart designer bag that identified her simply as Margaret Cerwin, M.D. No specialty was indicated. As she went to buy them another wine, Frank considered her smile. It was intriguing.

"What sort of physician are you?"

"Guess."

"Might you be a psychiatrist?"

"Very good," she said.

How had he guessed right? It might have been the knowing smile, distant yet confiding. The restrained availability was ever so slightly chilling. They talked about the concert. As they chatted she conveyed a warm familiarity with Mahler's music and with music in general. She also communicated, discreetly, a certain fascination with Bower.

"I'm very curious about you," she told him, "my friend."

He wanted to ask her how he could be her friend, but out of some polite instinct decided not to. In fact, he was at a loss for what to say next.

"Really?" he finally asked. "I'm not much of a mystery." But he allowed himself to suppose she saw him that way. He was, he knew, a rather handsome fellow, or at least a distinguished-looking one. He sometimes felt the charge of a woman's awareness. And everyone was a mystery. He felt unable to focus his thoughts, something akin to panic. Still, her manner encouraged him toward adventure. All at once he thought that whatever her coming to him might mean, he ought to live it out with her. At least for a while.

"You're wondering why I accosted you," she said. "I'll tell you why."

Her stare held him bound and silent.

"Life is short," she said. "At least it seems that way to me now. When I see someone who attracts me I try to meet them. I try to see what they have to say."

"Oh," he said. After a moment he asked her, "How do you choose people?"

"You mean, why you? Because you looked interesting. I

watched you listening. I may be a psychiatrist, but I'm a physiognomist too."

"Really?"

She smiled and looked away for a moment, then locked on him again. A humorous double take. It was a small felicity but dazzling. Her eyes shone, long-lashed, seeming barely to contain their own light.

"No. Not really. I don't think there are real physiognomists anymore. Maybe in China."

"You're always a step ahead of me."

"Am I? It's because I'm leading." Her artful arrogance was irritating, but the faint sting was sweet. "Actually, I prefer to be led."

Her smile troubled him. It was somehow familiar, secretive, imperturbable, maybe a little frosty. What it reminded him of, he realized, was the expression portrayed on very early Greek statuary.

"I need a ride," she said.

In the end, they left together, passing through the monumental entrance hall. On the way out they went by a bronze horseman rising from the saddle, brandishing a saber. The plate on its pedestal read ONE OF STUART'S VIRGINIANS. It was a tribute to wealthy, Confederately sympathetic old Baltimore.

They walked across the chill, darkened parking lot to his gray Camry. Bower opened the passenger door for her. He started the car and they sat looking straight ahead, past the vapor of their breath, visible against the headlights beyond the icing windshield. Bower put his seat belt on, and after a moment she did the same.

"Where to?" he asked.

She told him she had taken a taxi to the museum and she lived downtown. He drove them slowly out of the lot. They had driven a block south when he was aware of her fidgeting.

"You're going to think I'm insane," she declared.

He hastened to assure her. "No, no." In fact he experienced a little more anxiety about what might be coming.

"Going up to you as I did. I'm restless tonight."

"I suppose," Bower said, "I am too."

"I don't think I want to go home."

"Oh," said Bower.

"We could drive into the country a bit. To the hills. Or over the bridge."

"Let's take the bridge."

Bower had a house on the bay front of the Eastern Shore where he and his wife were planning to spend the weekend. He had not thought to go there, setting out from the museum. Nor even when he suggested the bridge. Now it occurred to him as a wanton possibility.

They put the lights of the city behind them and drove through icy rain. By the time they were on Route 13 the rain had stopped and the night sky was clearing. A wind from the ocean was driving rain clouds east across the bay to show a slivered late-October moon, unaccountably bright. There were stars.

"Oh," the woman, Margaret, exclaimed, "horns to the east."

"Excuse me?"

"Horns to the east. Haven't you heard it? Don't you know what it means?" Her questions seemed almost urgent. He was perplexed.

"No."

She laughed and recited,

> *Horns to the east,*
> *Soon be increased.*
> *Horns to the west,*
> *Soon be at rest.*

"Don't know?" she asked after a few seconds. "Can't you guess?"

"I don't think so," Bower said, wondering.

"Horns to the east," she said, "the waxing moon. Horns to the west, waning moon."

It took him a moment or two.

"Ah."

She mimicked him. "Ah! Ah is right."

"Did you make it up?" He got no answer. So he observed, "A Halloween moon."

"Just what I was thinking," she said.

When they turned off the highway she put an arm across the back of the seat.

"I wonder," she said playfully, "if we're going somewhere." He glanced at her and in the extraordinary light of the crescent moon saw again the archaic smile. "Where are we going?"

She, he thought, was the one who wanted to be led. He considered wildly, decided nothing. Then he said, "I have a house near Calverton."

"Really?"

"Yes, I do."

"I see. Could that be where we're going?"

"If you want to."

He was encouraged by her silence. Twenty minutes after they had passed through the decorous empty streets of old Chesterfield he pulled over to the shoulder. The road was wooded on both sides and it was possible to make out the POSTED signs on the near tree trunks. Then the persistent storm closed over the moonlit sky and it began to rain hard again.

"I have to make a call. Do you mind?"

"Certainly not."

He called his wife in Roland Park while Margaret sat stiffly beside him, listening equably, it seemed. He had not gotten out to make the call because of the rain. He looked into the dark dripping pine woods — anywhere but at his passenger — and declared to his wife he would be late. Offering no reason. When she asked for one he was reckless, a little unhinged by possibility.

"I felt out of sorts. I went for a drive in the country."

His wife asked if he was certain he was all right. He told her that, as far as that went, he was fine. When he turned to Margaret on the car seat beside him, he saw her bent forward, hands across her eyes as if in remorse or simply seeing no evil. He experienced another moment's panic. The wrong woman!

"Do you," he asked, "do you need to call anyone? I mean, to make a call?"

She shook her head and said nothing for the remainder of the ride. Shortly, they turned off onto a dirt road and followed its turns and doglegs past a few mailboxes at the head of dark driveways. The houses that showed lights were deep in the woods, far from the roadway. Overhead, the horned moon had appeared again, visible through bare wind-driven branches.

They parked in the clearing around Bower's house. Once out of the car they faced the salt-sour-scented gale off the bay. In the darkness they could hear its waves crashing against the unprotected shore. The house was shingled and square, a dignified practical house, unadorned except for a weathervane on the roof. It was impossible to see what the weathervane represented.

She had folded her arms and turned away from the wind. From her posture, Bower thought she seemed a little hesitant and subdued.

"Very nice," she said.

Bower pulled his own collar up against the chill. Now he was thrilled by his own impulsiveness and the stormy night sky, clearing again. Finally it seemed he was leading. He conducted them inside, his steadying hand lightly touching the sheath of leather that encased her. Bower turned on a lamp and raised the thermostat. Then, as she watched, he laid a fire and started it. His guest kept her coat on.

"Aren't you afraid of the house watch?"

"House watch? Not out here. A little more wine?" he asked her. "Madder music?"

The look she gave him was steady and flat, unamused. A little puzzled, slightly ashamed of his fit of brio, he went into the kitchen and opened a bottle of St. Emilion. He carried it out on a tray and poured for them.

"The good stuff this time," he said. She took a glass, but her look made him feel fat-witted and overcheery. "Like it?" he asked.

She only nodded without drinking. Suddenly it seemed the burden of discourse was his. She was looking, a little sadly, around the room.

"All these beautiful things," she said.

There were beautiful things in the room for people who knew how to look for them. Bower's wife collected early-American paintings and furniture. He had grown to appreciate them too. To keep the play of the evening alive, he began to give Margaret the tour.

The house itself was old, not quite Colonial but early nineteenth century. The front door opened directly on the living room, as it sometimes does in old houses. In that room stood a Mennonite chest with a sunburst painted on its front. The wall above it displayed a Kentucky quilt. The fireplace was equipped with fittings of old wrought iron. A table and chairs in a recessed dining area had the imperfect symmetry of rough joinery. Three of the wall paintings were genuine American primitives, and one was an attributed Robert Feke. Outside his computer workspace hung a later painting, a gloomy nightscape his wife thought might be an Albert Pinkham Ryder, but it lacked a provenance.

Margaret followed Bower's exposition of the room. She seemed to display little interest. From time to time she sipped the wine he had poured for her. Though the house had warmed, she kept her coat on.

"It's all very nice," she said, distantly polite.

"My wife has the eye," he said, as though Margaret were a casual guest and not the object of a particular seduction.

"Your wife? Isn't she afraid to leave all this out in the country? Isn't she afraid of losing what she has? Her house? Your attentions?"

Bower was very uncomfortable at having to explain his wife's personal qualities, but Margaret seemed to think she had a right to ask questions.

"What's here isn't all that valuable."

He watched Margaret set her empty wine glass on a place mat, sparing the finish of a dark mahogany table. A moment after setting it down, she touched the table's surface with two fingers and brought them away quickly, as if she were repelled by the dust on it.

"Oh," said Margaret, "I see." She looked around the room again. "What's her name? Would I like her?"

"I think so. Yes. I suppose. Her name is Jane."

"Jane. I'll bet I would."

"Please," Bower said, "take your coat off."

"I suppose she comes here with you?"

"Most weekends." He was growing impatient with her. "Is that some sort of problem?"

The look she gave him was again level, dead-eyed and stone-cold. He had rankled her. The antic animation of the last hours had somehow drained away.

"This isn't right," she said after a moment. "It would be wrong." She appeared suddenly stricken. "Another woman's bed!"

"What?" Though Bower knew her not at all, he thought there was a serious chance she might be joking.

"We can't," she said with surprising firmness.

"Oh."

"No, Frank. Sorry."

Bower was extremely disappointed. But edging his interior horizon, on a different quarter, appeared the faraway contours of relief. He tried to swallow the humiliation.

"You're a mercurial character. Aren't you?"

"Yes, I am," she said.

"I see."

"And here we are," she said. Suddenly she laughed, and for a moment she was lively and humorous again. "Out in the sticks. Don't you believe it's a woman's privilege to change her mind?"

"Oh, come on, Margaret." He was unsettled by her laughter and the cliché. She showed the expression he had learned to dread. The smile.

Driving her home was an embarrassment. He thought of switching on the car radio but decided it might only make things worse. Music would be irony. A stranger's voice would sound like mocking witness.

When they were back in the city, heading downtown along St. Paul Street, she told him brusquely that she lived in the Belvedere. It was an old hotel near the Washington Monument that had faded and then turned condo.

Margaret offered no goodbyes when they pulled up before the tastefully renovated entrance. They parted in the welter of Bower's shamed silence. Setting out for his own house in Roland Park, he kept his eyes on the road. As a result, he failed to see her climb into one of the cabs that always waited in front of the gay bar and club catty-corner to the Belvedere.

In the cab, Margaret made a call to her daughter. She was fatigued from the drive and irritable.

"Clean up, my dear."

Arriving, she found that Cordelia had cleaned up, after a fashion. At least there were no dishes in the sink. Nor was there — aside from a couple of withered apples, a moldering box of take-out rice, and a baby's bottle containing milk of indeterminate freshness — any food in the refrigerator.

"Christ, don't you eat?" Margaret asked.

"Yeah, I eat," Cordelia said, pouting. "How about you?"

Margaret inspected her.

"You don't look well."

"Oh, thanks," Cordelia said.

In Cordelia's room, Margaret found her grandson, diaper unchanged, lying uncomfortably with twisted covers and looking as though he had cried himself to sleep. As she stood there, the child awakened and whimpered.

"Wash that child and change him. How can you be so irresponsible?"

"All right, all right," Cordelia whined. Except for the petulant inflection, Cordelia had a cultivated voice like her mother's. In the bedroom, the baby cried savagely.

"Happy now?" asked Cordelia. She went into her room and slammed the door. Margaret took her sleek coat off and hung it carefully. Then she eased herself onto the living room sofa, took off her sensible shoes and put her feet up. She lay with her eyes closed, listening to the sounds from the next room, where Cordelia was alternately muttering to herself and crooning to the baby. After the child had been quiet for a while Cordelia came out, wearing her bomber jacket with its tombstone patch, ready to hit the street.

"Don't you think his eyes look odd?" Margaret said without rising.

"But he has beautiful eyes," Cordelia told her mother. "Angel eyes."

"You're slamming meth, aren't you, dear?"

Cordelia marched toward the apartment door, then turned in rage. Her mother cut off any reply.

"I've tried to persuade you. Your teeth will fall out. You'll age."

"Thanks again, Slim."

"I don't want to sit by and watch you lose your looks." She sat up to address her daughter. "And your mind. Tweakers are the most boring people. Who taught you to fix?"

"I knew how."

"No, baby. I'm sure it was Donny."

Cordelia opened the apartment door and started out.

"Just a moment, dearest. Where to? Leaving mother to babysit? Mother had a tough day."

"Really? Ball some poor dude?"

Margaret raised a despairing hand and waved off the insult. Leaving, Cordelia slammed the door, her second slammed door of their brief evening. Margaret brooded for a while and then decided to call Cordelia's dearest friend. Some people actually called him Slash, but to Margaret he had always been just Donny.

"Hey, Donny." She tried to keep her voice low for the infant's sake. "How's tricks?"

"Yo, Slim," Donny said cautiously.

"Could it be that you've just instructed my baby in the art of slamming?"

"No way. She's a big girl. Either way, see what I'm saying, she gets more independent."

"Are you hearing me, Donno? Don't you dare treat Cordy like some skeeza. I'm cross."

"I hear you," Donny admitted.

"Good. Because if you ever turn my daughter out, I think I'll kill you."

"You are paranoid," Slash told her as firmly as possible. "You're, like, saying things."

Margaret paused to let him reflect on how thin the joke was.

"On a happier note," she said, "I have a joint for us. I've identified this awful man. House full of good things. So be here tomorrow midmorning and don't be hammered. Or is that a vain hope and it has to drop without you?"

"I'm there."

"Okay, and bring my daughter back here. I can't spend all day babysitting. I have a meet with the Smiling Lascar tomorrow."

The man Margaret called the Smiling Lascar was a South Asian pharmacist in Bethesda with whom she could trade in pseudoephedrine. Victor moved it out to some country cousins in West Virginia who cooked it into pseudo-crystal for distribution by bike clubs around the upper South. Victor's overextended family was basically a criminal enterprise, and through him Margaret could maintain a phantom presence from the D.C. suburbs to the remotest hollow and never consort with ruffians.

She did undertake a little discreet consorting, though. Exploiting the average psychopath's lack of social confidence, she was able to reach out past Donny to his own network and had already stolen a number of his supporters out from under him. Their shabby world was often exhilarating — the commerce in ginseng and bear livers, actual moonshine from traditional stills, marijuana, arms and ammunition, cars, speed, motorcycles. Donny's associates seemed to think they rightfully owned all motorcycles, as the Masai thought they owned all cattle. These men, she thought, were irreplaceable, the sons of the pioneers. She even had a certain secret fondness for Slash and understood her daughter's attraction. Still, she considered him needy.

"So you'll take care of that, no? And you'll bring a rental truck and plates? And you want gray coveralls or some neutral color."

"You got it, Slim," said Donny Slash.

"And you'll bring Cordy over here? And you'll show up? Scout's honor? Because this thing needs to be tomorrow."

"I'll come over too, yeah. I haven't seen much of Little Jimmy."

It was annoying the way he constantly referred to the baby as Littlejimmy, as though it were all one snively word. He had got Cordelia doing it. He had not seen much of the child because Margaret had various means of keeping him away.

"No, you haven't," she said.

"I mean, hey. This is my child here."

"Certainly, Donny," Margaret told him. "If you say so."

And that was that, and so, she thought, to bed. But no, the phone began its song and dance, and she had Kimmie on the line. Kimmie was Margaret's schoolgirl chum and former patient.

"Oh, Kimmie," she said. "It's so late."

Kimmie was a professor of composition at a small women's college in New England and a published poet. Margaret had been visiting with her on a business and shopping trip to the Northeast.

"Margaret!" Kimmie said breathlessly. "Did you take my car? My car is utterly gone. Vanished from the driveway."

"We discussed this, Kimmie."

"We did?"

"We certainly did. I borrowed it to drive to the train. I left it at the station. How can you not remember?"

She and Kimmie had planned to shop for early-American art and antiques along New York Route 22. Arriving, Margaret had found her friend, who was seriously bipolar, in a state approaching raving mania. To punish her, Margaret had taken Kimmie's battered '65 Ford Mustang and driven it to D.C. in partial payment to the Smiling Lascar.

"At the station? But I'm stranded. I'm marooned, you see, and I can't . . ."

"It's autumn break, Kimmie. You don't need to go anywhere." In the end, she had simply to insist. Kimmie had forgotten about the loan as a result of her medication. Or of not taking it. Or something. After a while she pressed the red button on Kimmie and switched the phone off. Then she checked on young Jim and went to bed.

It was midmorning when Cordelia and Slash arrived. Margaret looked them over in their bib overalls and work shirts. Cordelia's getup fit badly. She wore a Depression-style gray tweed cap turned backward.

"You're late. I hope you brought everything?" Then she performed a stylized double take. "By the way, your mustache is rat-like," she told Donny. "What have you done to it?"

Donny Slash, who had come in wearing a suave, cheery

smile, lost his composure. He was always trying to impress Margaret favorably. But Margaret's secret attraction to him was a gratuitous grace over which he had no control at all.

"Whattya mean, Slim?"

"Never mind."

Cordelia giggled. The twisted relationship between her mother and Slash amused her.

"I've identified this awful man," Margaret explained. She meant she had acquired bits and pieces of the Bowers' life and documents from an addicted antiques runner who had become aware of Mrs. Bower's collection. The man saw the Bowers regularly at auctions. On the day after Margaret's return from Kimmie's, the runner had spotted Bower at the museum and called her. Although Margaret had actually been a psychiatrist, her name was not Cerwin.

"By the way, Cordy, are you whacked, my darling?" She turned on Donny, who fidgeted and blinked under Margaret's fierce glance. Blinking was his shot at showing an honest countenance.

"Fuck no!" Cordelia said.

"Fuck no? Because your lips are purple. And your friend!" She addressed Donny with a humorless smile. "You're whacked also. And you smell of beer. You're drunk. You've both been up all night slamming crystal. God bless us and save us!"

"No, man," said Donny. "We're cool. We're down."

"Cool? How cool you're cool, you moron!"

"Hey, Slim, man," Donny said, repentant, "it's all good."

"Do you know what this means?" Margaret asked. "It means we'll have to call Desirée." Desirée was a Haitian girl who often minded the baby. "I'll have to cancel the Lascar. I'll have to expose my posterior on the open road. You can't drive." She turned on Cordelia. "Cordy can't drive. She has warrants. Oh, God," she moaned, "the two of you."

"Don't let her come!" Cordelia implored Donny. "It's such a drag when she comes."

"Yeah, sure," Slash said.

"Well, it is," said Cordelia savagely. "Mother." She pronounced the word with the irony of the street.

"Shame on you," Margaret said. "And take off that stupid hat."

It was close to noon when they arrived in Calverton and parked on the road a few yards up from the Bowers' house. Margaret looked as chic as a middle-aged woman in white coveralls ever could, but she was annoyed at the delays.

"Check it out."

Slash started out of the truck.

"Not you," Margaret told him. "Cordy."

Cordy returned to say that the coast was clear.

"No system?" Slash asked.

Margaret laughed bitterly, snorted. "He didn't set it. People like him often don't."

They drove up to the house.

"Even if they'd set the system," said Donny, "I coulda disarmed it."

"Yes, you're wonderful, Slash," Margaret said. She addressed him as Slash only to torment him. "Now check the weathervane." She indicated the metal instrument on the roof. It had the form of a killer whale and was handsomely wrought.

"Nice," said Donny.

"Nice. So can you?"

"Sort of a hassle. But yeah." He turned and looked down the wooded driveway behind them. "Think it's cool?" From somewhere in the middle distance they heard the whine of a chain saw. Someone cutting firewood. Cordelia, without her bomber jacket or tweed cap, was jumping up and down out of high spirits and to keep warm.

"Let it go," Margaret told him. "Maybe we can take it when we're weathervane shopping. Open the door, please."

"Deadbolt?"

"He didn't use two keys."

Slash tried and failed to open the door with a credit card. Then he applied the Halligan bar his cousins had stolen from a West Virginia state police car. The door, lopsidedly, fell open.

"Open fuckin' sesame! Perfecto Garcia!"

Margaret brushed past him and the couple followed her. Inside, they put on their rubber gloves and took up items as Margaret directed. As she watched through a window, they carried furniture and bric-a-brac outside and stashed it in the rental truck on padded mover's quilts.

"*Doucement*," Margaret advised them. "Gently."

After their exertions her two assistants both began to tremble with cold and the drug.

"Let's go," Cordelia whined. She had begun jumping again, in the Bowers' living room, and was working herself into a state. "Let's go before some asshole comes. Like joggers or . . ."

Donny, annoyed, grabbed her arm to hush her and discourage her bouncing. Cold as it was, they watched Margaret unbutton her leather coat and take a pearl-handled straight razor from one of the pockets and hasten into the bathroom. Very shortly she emerged. Her face was contorted with what appeared to be rage.

"Let's go, Slash," Cordelia said, pulling him toward the door.

They stood just outside the crippled, half-open door. They could hear Margaret screaming inside, the smash of glass and crockery, the rending of cloth.

"What?" he demanded. "What the fuck?"

"You've never seen her do this before? This is like her signature mode." She moved from the door with an expression of pity and distaste. "Oh, Jesus, I hate it."

"Does what? What's she doing?"

"You'll find out."

Slash stepped inside and came out again.

"Jeez," he said, "she's cuttin' it up pretty good. She's wired. Bad."

Cordelia shook her head and sighed impatiently.

"Yeah, she's like loot and pillage."

He and Cordelia stood shivering, watching the driveway, until Margaret appeared. She looked quite composed, if a little unsteady and breathing audibly. Donny and Cordelia said nothing.

"Okay," Margaret said. "*Tout fini*. Let's roll."

They had driven the truck only a few miles along the highway when Donny saw a flashing bluey in his rearview mirror. A startling burst of siren rose and fell. Cordelia, crouching behind the seats, cursed and moaned.

"What?" Donny asked Margaret.

"Were you speeding?"

"No way."

"Well, pull over." She turned back to Cordelia. "Relax, dear. We'll survive."

The cruiser that had pulled them over belonged to the town cops. There was only one of them, quite a young man. He wore cheap sunglasses, so Margaret could not be sure how stupid he was.

"I only wear handcuffs when I'm being fucked," Margaret whispered. She was joking to encourage them. The cop got out and stood just to the rear of the driver's side door, looking in at Cordelia.

"License and registration," he told Donny. Donny had a forged but well-made Virginia driver's license. The cop gave them all the once-over and stepped back and away to read the documents. He did not return them. From her side, Margaret leaned across Slash to address the young policeman.

"A problem, officer?"

He looked at her without apparent expression.

"Where you all coming from?"

"From Princeton, New Jersey," Margaret declared. "Actually, we're on our way home."

"Where to?"

"Across the bay. I have a house in Fredericksburg."

"What about you, sir?" the cop asked Slash.

"Little Creek, Virginia. See, we're driving her. Moving some furniture." He was blinking stupidly in all directions. Margaret gave him an elbow.

"Didn't take Ninety-five?"

"Thirteen is so much more pleasant," said Margaret. "Sometimes faster, too."

The cop turned on Cordelia in her lair behind the seats. "That true?"

"Yes, it is," Cordelia answered, sounding like her mother.

"This lady your mom?"

"Yes, she is."

"You family too?" the officer asked Donny.

"No," Donny said. He showed the officer his top-of-the-line smile. "Hired help."

"That right?" he asked the ladies.

"Well, yes," Margaret answered a bit impatiently. After a moment the officer handed Donny the registration and license.

"Have a nice day, ma'am." He took a last glance at Donny Slash. "Drive carefully, sir."

When the cop had vanished from sight, Donny and Cordelia whooped with joy.

"Oh, Moms! You're like so great!" She was, in the end, her mother's greatest admirer.

"Hey, Slim," Donny yelled. "You're awesome, man."

He took one hand off the wheel to offer Margaret a high-five. She condescended to return it.

"Everybody loves you when you're somebody else," she explained.

The Wine-Dark Sea

....

O N   A   V E R Y   F O G G Y   late-autumn morning, a man named Eric Floss was wandering the quaint streets of a preserved Connecticut whaling town. He found himself walking scrubbed brick sidewalks that fronted the marble steps of exquisite Federal-style houses. Old ironwork bordered gardens grown with lilac bushes and hedged in boxwood. There were warmly lighted shops soon to open for the sale of antique ornamental pieces and vintage furniture. One place had antique willow-patterned china from the ginseng trade. Most of the windows, though, offered midlevel, tourist-standard marine studies. There was scrimshaw from the lathes of the Philippines and here and there some genuine old pieces, crude but authentic. A few shops had rows of jade and amber jewelry for sale and the odd lissome ivory apsara.

Floss had come to the town because it was where a ferry crossed many times a day to Steadman's Island, the only habitable point on a reef of rocky islands, a low-key resort where large holdings and a paucity of space and fresh water had made summering expensive and restricted. One section of Steadman's Island was called Heron's Neck, the site of the island's largest and most ornate summer cottage. The big houses were all called cottages.

It had become generally known that the owner of Heron's Neck, a friend of the Secretary of Defense, had made the place available to his friend for a few days. The Secretary liked to summon his political retainers to remote and inconvenient meeting sites to inform them of his wishes, and the island had become a favorite. That fall week he had called a conference to sic the dogs of his department on some of their opposite numbers in other government agencies.

Eric was a freelancer whose demonstrated unreliability had limited his prospects of journalistic advancement. It was not his reporting or the soundness of his prose that had failed to satisfy, but his tendency to overlook deadlines and even entire assignments once undertaken. This time he had signed for an article on the reaction of the year-round island population to the presence of the policy conference on its shores. The journal was a post-pornographic monthly that had passed into the hands of an old colleague of his. That fall, both Eric and the magazine were attempting to find their way back to seriousness. The magazine was cutting back on its ration of sexual fantasy and hard-core pix, running an occasional piece of political revelation. Eric had nearly stopped drinking and using recreational drugs.

The theory behind the story was that the locals might have some comments worth recording on the combination of mystery and ostentation that surrounded such a high-level, high-security event. Moreover, Eric had what he thought might be a useful local connection. One of the year-round inhabitants, Annie Shumway, was the sister of a woman with whom Eric had traveled in the Middle East. It would be an interesting beginning, he thought, to visit them.

The fact was that his enthusiasm for the story had been waning since he had pitched it successfully to his acquaintance. Still, he thought that if he went to the island something original might present itself. And he would get to see the place and meet Lou's sister. There were no hotels, and both of the bed-and-breakfasts were serving as barracks for the security detail. So he had rallied some effrontery and telephoned Annie, who had, with obvious reluctance, invited him to dinner with her husband and herself.

He was a few weeks out of rehab in southern California, but contrary to its principles he had started smoking the odd joint and getting drunk by six. He had occasional blackouts once more and woke up with strange troublesome women. Still, he had allowed himself to believe that things were working out. Hanging around the classy mainland town, waiting for the next ferry, Eric found the fog, particularly, beginning to bother him.

On the Atlantic side of the island stood a cluster of small saltbox houses where the original farming village of Stead-man's Island had been. Some of the houses were as old as the first settlement, and some were new, conforming to the original style. A few barns there had been converted to condos, over ineffectual opposition. Among the most vigorous opponents of the condos — of all exploitive change — were the Shumways, Annie and Taylor, who lived in one of the saltboxes. Taylor Shumway's family went back on the island for centuries. Annie, his wife, came from Oregon, where they had met at a seminar for eco-activists. Annie was not in her first youth, but no one would quite call her middle-aged. She was youthful, peppy and attractive. She wrote a gardening column in the island paper every week and taught two primary grades at the school.

That evening, she and Taylor were expecting Eric Floss, an old boyfriend of her sister Lou's, who had called out of nowhere. He was at the ferry on the mainland, waiting for a crossing. The piggy conference of fat cats on the Neck and the impossible visibility had stalled all transport. Eric claimed to be an alternative journalist who wanted to keep one eye on the conference. "One eye," he had said.

In the late afternoon, fog had settled so thickly over the island that it was difficult to see across the main street of the village or even the neighboring houses. The fog warning at Salvage Reef, off the northeast light, sounded at sixty-second intervals. Annie had never found anything dismal about the groaning of the horn. But in the faded gray light of that afternoon she had an unfamiliar sense of enclosure and isolation. She had never experienced so many days at the heart of such enveloping fog before. At the same time the air was wet and sweet with honeysuckle, bay and wild rose, maybe more fragrant for being confined.

She had been taken by surprise by the sudden necessity of entertaining a guest, a situation she shamefacedly knew she had brought on herself. The Shumways were not dinner-party people. Taylor Shumway, who worked on the ferry, kept a boat and lobster traps; his days began well before autumn light. Annie Sorenson-Shumway did not drink, and Taylor couldn't. He particularly did not enjoy company at home. On her side, Annie was indifferent. She had plenty of social life around her Sunday Meeting, the island school and her botany column in the weekly paper. For Taylor, a pleasurable group activity after work might be driving across the island with his power jacks to help a crew raise the corner of a house. He would leave before the beer was opened.

But that morning, after Eric had made clear who he was, she had impulsively invited him for dinner. He seemed to have sort of expected it, and she was a bit of a people pleaser. Then too, she was plain curious about any guy Lou had taken up with — Looie was a world traveler and collector of what she called "types," but the individuals Annie had met seemed pretty unique. She was also curious about what Eric was on to, as a freelance journalist, in terms of the big-shot gathering on the Neck. She and Taylor had both been activists. Taylor had gone to prison, though it was only drinking that had moved him to hurt anyone.

Annie realized that if Taylor had answered the telephone, he would have told Eric Floss to piss off, or to do something along those lines. She herself had been amazed when Eric had patently angled for shelter. But she had offered him the couch. What else could a civilized person do?

"What the shit?" Taylor had demanded when she reached him between ferry trips.

His manner got her back up, and of course she felt foolish.

"Well, gee," she said, "people dropping in. That used to be all right."

"When was that?" he asked.

On the mainland, Eric paced Harbor Street, trying not to look at his watch too often. Dead time was hard for him. His recent rehabilitation had been partly paid for by a prosperous former girlfriend, a television producer, who had sent him for treatment at her favorite facility. They had treated him at Possibilities for what she called virtual addiction. She used the word "virtual" in the old journalistic way, as a nifty reinforcing adjective. However, Eric's addictions were substantial, to marijuana, alcohol and so on. The docs at Possibilities had pronounced him bipolar, a condition formerly known as manic depression. He had then been virtually imprisoned with loons, and a very expensive confinement it was.

Possibilities was well named, since anything could happen to you there, from being whacked with a chair leg in a locked corridor by a brother or sister bipolaroid to a lightning-fast heave-ho if your money ran out. The idea was to accentuate the positive, eliminate the negative, and you became Mr. or Ms. In Between. There were pills to zonk or stun. There were even pills to encourage, but Eric was not allowed them. Dope was around, but of course getting thrown out was a waste of time and money. Eric managed not to use it. Hitting the street, he had felt ready for sobriety. Some unremembered misstep had betrayed him into his own lower nature.

Annie, the Steadman's Island lady he had spoken to — importuned somewhat — sounded nicer than her sister. Anyway, Eric was used to soliciting contacts and hospitality in a variety of places. For quite a few years he had been traveling the world, scratching a living from his trade. He had written about the Caribbean, Southeast Asia and the Middle East and had seen disturbing things along the way. At times he had experienced the elation of being in new cities and new landscapes that were dangerous and fascinating. As a younger man he had been able to truly rejoice in those things.

In the early afternoon, Eric found his way to the comfortably unpreserved back streets of town. In the shadow of a fog-wrapped railroad underpass he came on a tavern called the Fisher's Inn. It had an anchor over the door, always a good sign. The place was empty except for a couple of old-timers in ragged team jackets and baseball hats. At the Fisher's Inn, where no one bought drinks for Eric, the fog seen through dim windows was seamless. Eric sauntered out and took up headquarters in a yo-ho netting-and-knotboard joint that overlooked the water, or would have if there had been anything to see through the gray shroud. He was waiting for the hour when the public might be carried across the bay. Beefeater was prohibitively expensive in the harbor spot, but Eric allowed himself several. He had drunk more modestly at the Inn. On the walk to the dock he had been shocked to discover two joints of the finest pakalolo in his raincoat pocket. A left hand had faked out the right again.

In a day or two, the conferees at Heron's Neck would hold a press conference on their deliberations at a media center on the mainland. From Eric's point of view, the only interesting thing about the event were the rumors of the

Secretary's spectacular mood swings. Insider material, not funny if you were a ragged peasant in the shadow of his gleaming wings. Not funny for his undermanned, under-equipped and underinformed legions either. A few insiders had suggested in print that the main event of the conference might be some maneuvering by the Secretary's enemies to test his grip on things. There would be leaks — controlled burns, as they said in the Forest Service. That kind of thing, even considering Eric's perspective, was hard to resist.

Security officials had canceled a bird census for the duration of the conference, not that anyone could see a bird that week. It was a gesture by the Secretary's office. They were contemptuous of the sort of folks who might object to the cancellation, as they imagined such people. Around the Secretary's office they imagined such people a lot, and felt certain that the fine, all-believing yeomanry they claimed to represent hated such people as much as they did.

The trip over to Steadman's was agonizingly slow. The small two-deck ferry proceeded through swells that presented a glassy surface but set the boat into long fore-and-aft glides. The dope was good for nausea, so Eric found himself a gear box and let the breeze carry his smoke over the wake. There was nothing to be seen except the water; everything else was invisible, even the squawking gulls that attended the ferry. When, after an hour and a half, the boat eased into the island's principal town, Eric had no idea what the place looked like. His first sight of the island as the ferry came about to tie up was of Feds in raincoats on the dock, backed up by armed Navy men in jump suits. He flicked his roach into the harbor.

The houses of town were white clapboard, and there were a couple of old buildings with cupolas out of Currier and Ives. Putting the place together was akin to a blind person's feeling out an elephant, so thick was the going. It was not so hard to find a liquor store. There, a glum Portuguese man sold him two bottles of California cabernet for an all-time record price. The wine would be his house offering, one he ought to have bought off-island. He bought cigarettes too, Marlboros, the red-and-white packs that had once bought taxi rides across emerging nations. These also cost a lot.

The liquor store clerk gave him directions to the Shumways' house, which turned out to be not far but an uphill trudge. He was a little unsteady on the way. After a few minutes of walking he turned to look down on the harbor, but of course it had disappeared behind him. No up, he thought. Neither down nor sideways. It was liberating, the complete obscurity. Past gone, present solitary, future fading out. A crazy little whoop of joy inside. Must be a rush, he thought.

At twelve-step meetings and to nurturing females Eric liked to give the impression that dreadful sights had brought him to the booze- and drug-examined life. He liked, in fact, to give himself the same impression.

In his heart he knew better than to blame his ways on bad experience. No one would convince him that character was fate; he had seen too much of each to believe it. Everyone was tempted by bad choices great and small, everyone was subject to bad luck. But he had always been a boozy, druggy person, and he would have been one had he lived to middle age in the bosom of mercy itself.

All at once he thought he heard laughter, somewhere distant, at the heart of the fog. Laughter and convivial chat, a strong sound carrying many voices. Something about it made him shudder. Then the voices were subsumed in the rattle of dead leaves underfoot and his interior noises. For all he could tell the laughter had started there. Listening for whatever it was, he became aware of the foghorn on the island. He had been hearing foghorns for hours. He incautiously took the second joint out, turned from the breeze and lit it for two quick tokes.

After a few minutes the slope evened out and the blacktop road he followed looked recently surfaced. He saw that there was an old house on his right, fronted by moss-covered old stone, and beyond that a sagging porch with a defunct oil furnace sitting on it. There was a light on in the back. He walked on and saw more houses, widely spaced on both sides of the road. They appeared and disappeared behind him. Then he heard singing, the real thing, a single voice.

Steps on, he came upon a young woman in gardening gloves cutting and gathering flowers, pulling clumps of nettle and pigweed as she worked. She was tall and pretty with graying black hair. No kid was she, but she seemed very youthful.

She looked up and saw him step out of the fog and put a hand to her hair, which was to him — as they said at AA — a trigger. Her eyes were blue, her look unguarded. She seemed to be shy and sweet and much nicer than his former girl-friend.

"Hi, Annie," he said to her. "Eric." They shook hands. "What kind of flowers?"

Annie had chosen mainly asters, zinnias and gerbera daisies, all of them dripping wet. Gathering flowers, which was something Annie did all season long, never failed to remind her of the days in her childhood when she was appalled at cutting them at all. She was practically ten before she could truly believe that they did not experience pain. The thought came back to her in various forms, borne on different memories.

She told him with a smile what kind they were. "I always think they have feelings," she said.

As she straightened up, he asked, "You think the flowers have feelings?"

"Well, not really." She brushed the soil and stems from her hands and smiled.

A chatterbox, he thought. Goofy like Lou, the ex.

"I understand. Too much pain, right?"

Annie affected to laugh heartily and turned away, blushing, toward the door. Eric followed her inside.

Taylor was sipping apple juice from a fruit jar at the kitchen table.

"This is Taylor, Eric," Annie told him.

"Neat," Eric said, glancing at the fireplace, at Taylor, and at the fifty-year-old furniture that had never made its way back to the mainland.

Annie hastened to display the garden flowers to her husband. "What do you think of these, Taylor? They'll work, don't you think?"

Taylor looked over his uninvited guest and burped rudely. He stared at the backpack Eric was removing.

"Good of you to join us, there, Eric."

Eric laughed as politely as he could.

A garlicky vegetable stew Taylor had made days before was simmering on the stove. "Eric is Lou's ex," said Annie.

"I heard," said Taylor.

Though he had passed forty that very summer, there was a quality about Taylor of late lingering adolescence. He kept staring at Eric's backpack.

Outside the kitchen window that looked on Annie's befogged garden, a male cardinal was fiercely attacking his own reflection in the glass. The cardinal was searching for a mate and was determined to drive off rivals. He had become obsessed by the house's windows; a tireless challenger kept appearing in them, matching him cry for cry, dealing him hurtful thumps. The bird's every sally was checked by this relentless enemy. But the love-driven red bird had heart. For days, from misty dawn until the dissolving of the light it had been fighting itself. Annie and Eric looked toward the window.

"Sad," Annie said.

"That's life, isn't it?" Eric said, turning to Taylor. Taylor looked at him without expression.

"It shouldn't be," Annie said.

Annie and Eric turned back to the window and then took a sneaking look at each other.

"Speaking of how life ought to be," Eric said after a moment, "I have some wine for us."

Annie blushed again.

"We don't . . ." she began.

"We don't drink it," Taylor said sharply. He stood up as Eric took his two bottles of cabernet out of the bag and put them on the table. Taylor took a pair of metal-rimmed glasses from his blue chambray shirt pocket. Then he picked up one bottle after the other and examined them.

"God damn, man," he said softly. He was looking at the price stickers over the labels.

One thing Annie had learned to live with was Taylor's anger. In her case, that anger threatened only her peace of mind because Taylor never hit her. He had, however, served twenty-three months in an Oregon state prison for an act of violence. During the period when she and Taylor had been eco-activists in the Northwest, he had responded to a taunt from a local logger. The response caused him to become one of the few individuals in that state ever charged, under an old frontier law, with the crime of mayhem, which the movement lawyers were able to plead down from felonious assault. Taylor's removable dental bridge had caused disfiguring damage to the logger's nose. Taylor was passionate, and in certain situations he could lose control. Situations involving alcohol were dangerous for him and for others.

"God damn, man," he said again, and smiled. He had never replaced the bridge.

Taylor stood a couple of inches taller than Eric. Thin and tanned, he managed to look frail in spite of his size. He was long-necked, floating a prominent Adam's apple. His eyes were blue and bright. It was impossible not to notice the humps of muscle on his narrow shoulders and the rippling of sinew down the length of his tanned bony arms. He would never look exactly athletic, but the work he did as a deckhand on the island ferry had made him extremely strong. His hands were scarred and callused, the knuckles battered, split, fractured and healed over. He showed a high forehead, prominent cheekbones and a strong jaw. His fair hair was as soft and fine as a girl's, cut short and lying slack on the top of his skull like a tonsured knight's. Annie's sister, Lou, had described him as an ectomorph, a word previously unknown to Annie. It apparently meant a tall, skinny guy who brooded and couldn't drink. That was Taylor.

"Thanks, Eric," Annie hastened to say. "We don't drink wine."

Taylor thrust one of the bottles under Annie's nose to show her what the wine cost. Like everything else on the island, the wine was grossly overpriced. Taylor laid the bottle lengthwise on the table and rolled it casually toward where Eric was standing. Annie made a move to catch it if it fell.

"Wow!" she said. "Thanks anyway," she told Eric kindly. The prices were a little disgusting given the state of the world, but he had only meant to be polite.

"Waste of money," said Taylor. Annie saw that he might be at the point of tossing them outside, breaking them. But Eric had a corkscrew out. He took one of the bottles straight from Taylor's hand and uncorked it.

"Guess I'll have to drink them both then," said Eric, grinning.

Mainly to distract Taylor, Annie hastened to bring Eric a fruit jar.

"He'll just piss it out," Taylor said. "Won't you, Eric?"

"Ah!" Eric said. "But first the buzz! Right, Annie?" He raised his fruit jar to her.

It made Annie dizzy to watch him drain it. Of course it had been a mistake to let him crash at the house — she had known as much at the time. It had been a bad day for Taylor because there had been special trips for big shots on the ferry. Fog had grounded planes.

"Hey, let's eat!" she said with feigned delight. Taylor belched again, set his juice on the table and shambled to the stove. Annie watched him as though she were forcing him there by her will. "Veggie stew," she declared, "always better the second or third day." She looked at Eric, trying to convey anxiety, a warning, something to make him cool it.

Eric poured himself more wine, drank it and stood up.

"Going out for a smoke," he explained. "Be a second." He took the wine with him.

"What?" Taylor asked loudly.

Outside, the breeze seemed only to turn the enveloping fog on itself. The air was sweet. Eric felt excited but confused. What was with the looks Annie was giving him? Did she have a clue how lovely she looked with her guileless Oregon-blue eyes? She seemed innocent but mysterious. Clearly the husband was a menace. He was in danger.

In recent years Eric had tried to internalize a mechanism that controlled his impulsiveness. But he had gone on drinking and smoking too much dope, traveling too much. Strange thoughts assailed him. In Haiti, it might have been, or Indonesia — somewhere that powerful, perhaps infernal, supernatural beings roamed — he dreamed that an unmanageable spirit had entered into him. Flashbacks? Second adolescence on the way down? One never knew.

He smoked one Marlboro after another. Turning toward the Shumways' door, he thought, Make an entrance! An inappropriate urge, like so many. He opened the door dramatically to face them. Annie looked alarmed. Eric marched to the table and opened the second bottle of wine.

"Hey," he said. "Sorry, bad habit."

"Well," she said, "it reheats."

Taylor served the stew in silence, a somnambulist waiter. Eric noticed that the cardinal's struggles continued into darkness. He thought that unusual.

"Veggies, right?" Eric asked them. "Love 'em! Never eat anything with a face. Seriously," he asked them, "I mean, what is meat? A certain consistency to the teeth. A rub for the gums. Like chomp chomp, right? No more to it. Hey, guys," Eric said, "how about some more plonkorino?" He poured some into his fruit glass. "Overpriced? Yes! And yet? Not so bad."

Taylor had begun to smile unpleasantly. Eric looked at the plate before him. He took a forkful of the vegetable stew and put it in his mouth, as much to silence himself as anything else. He glanced at Annie. She seemed strangely calm.

"Hey, Eric," Taylor said finally, "why don't you tell us what you're really doing out here." Eric shrugged and kept his eyes on his plate and swallowed. "He's a wanderer," Taylor told his wife.

A wanderer, Eric thought. That was a good one. "The conference," he said. "At Heron's Neck."

"You ain't part of that shit, are you?"

"No." Eric tried to explain. "I came out to see . . . what local people had to say."

"Local people?" Taylor asked. "What do you mean by that?"

"He doesn't mean anything," Annie said.

"I got nothing to say," Taylor told him. "Annie's got nothing to say neither."

"I might, Taylor."

"I should have been here earlier," Eric explained. "Fog. And I had you guys' address from Lou. And I wanted to maybe meet her friends. So I thought I'd call and say hi. So here I am. Tomorrow . . ."

"On your merry way?" Annie Shumway asked. "Up to the Neck and the conference? Hey, this ratatouille turned out really well."

"Well, no," Eric said.

She was watching Eric being overcome by the wine. He was ever so slightly like Taylor. Like her dad too, though not quiet and surely not violent. These people shouldn't drink. Like her dad. Scandinavian family on her side. Surely not violent, but you could never tell. She had discovered once that drunks were boring and unpleasant, and she had left Taylor once, before they lived on the island. Then the guy she had gone with had told her: Boy, that asshole — meaning Taylor — was work. He was your job, not a lot more than that. She had thought, Oh, I don't know. Because he, that guy, was also boring and unpleasant, and violent sometimes himself, not as brave as Taylor, and that turned out to count with her, as it did with most women. He was not committed to the world outside himself the way Taylor was.

She got tired of the guy mocking Taylor; she came to see it as mockery against herself. So love has no pride like the song says, and she had found out how ruthless she could be in a worthy cause, and she had gone back to Taylor, who took her back quite lovingly. They had moved to the island, and she had made people unhappy and she had helped people and she thought helping felt better, as was well known. So that was love for Annie.

"Veggies pretty good," she told the men. "Very nice, Taylor."

"The bird life is interesting here too." The word for Taylor's smile, Eric thought, was grim. Unless he had started imagining it, the cardinal was still at the window. "You a bird watcher too?" the grim ferryman asked. "You know," he asked his wife, "you remember the last pack of weird bird watchers we had?" He turned the rictus back on its subject. "They were Feds, Eric. They were government spies. Now, you say you're here for that conference. You say you're talking to local people. What's up, partner?"

"Well, not really." Eric proposed to explain himself further.

"Maybe you know something we don't, Eric."

Perhaps because of the bird outside, the dark Paraclete descended on Eric once again.

"Know something you don't?" He turned to Annie with a radiant countenance, then to Taylor. "That may be."

Taylor trembled.

"Taylor probably doesn't believe a lot of what he reads in the papers," Eric ventured, addressing Annie.

"You got that right," said Taylor. "I disregard the trash."

Annie watched, less anxiously. Having seen these situations before helped. Fraught as they got, they usually ended with some bloodless antler-rattling when she rallied herself to protect Taylor's feckless prey.

Eric had fallen under the spell of his demon.

"This is wise," he said. "It's not just a matter of slanted perspective. It's a matter of arrant fictionalizing. They rarely get caught."

"He says it himself!" Taylor declared. "Admits it's all bull-shit!"

"I've never heard it put that way, Taylor, have you?" Annie asked. "I want to hear." And she did, if she could not change the subject.

"Like those planes!" Taylor did not raise his voice but spoke with great passion. "That was faked, wasn't it? The planes into buildings. For oil, wasn't it?"

"There were no planes," Eric said.

"But wait," Annie exclaimed.

"I knew it!" Taylor shouted. He half rose from his chair. "No planes whatsoever!"

"No, Taylor," Eric said. "No planes." The force within him drove him to assume a wise condescending expression. An air, perhaps, of punditry. "Annie? There were no planes, do you understand?"

"But people were killed," Annie said. Taylor, triumphant, only grew more angry.

"Annie? Taylor? Have either of you ever heard of fractal imaging?"

"I have," Annie said. "I think." Taylor looked as though he were hearing something he had always known without quite realizing it.

"Did you know," Eric asked, "that in professional wres-tling the outcome was always agreed to? The referee called the signals. This did not mean that people didn't get hurt." Eric chuckled. "Oh yes, Annie, people got hurt. Even killed. Did you know that the former Soviet People's Army ac-cepted a four percent casualty rate in maneuvers?"

"This wasn't the Russians," Taylor said. "This was no ma-neuver."

Eric looked at the empty fruit jar and spoke thoughtfully. "That depends, Taylor, on what you mean by a maneuver. Think about it."

"What are you trying to do, man," Taylor asked, "make some bullshit excuse or something?"

"No no no, Taylor, don't misunderstand."

Annie watched Eric carefully. Taylor took a deep breath and puffed through closed lips. Eric leaned backward in his uneven captain's chair with an air of complacency.

"Watch the chair, Eric," Annie warned, but Eric took no notice.

"I've been doing this all my professional life, my two friends. I've been — you might say — behind the scenes. Listen to your Uncle Eric, as I'll call myself tonight. Whatever you think is happening, be certain it's not happening. Nothing you ever see or hear is correct. Shit, it's not even real. See, some are content. Others confused. Some shocked into a dreadful unprotesting silence. Some incensed, filled with impotent rage. All persuaded."

"I'll give you impotent rage," Taylor said softly.

"It's a funny idea," Annie said. "But our rage isn't impotent at all, I'm afraid. Although," she said to Taylor, "we're very peaceful people. We've accepted peace."

"You!" Taylor kept his seat but turned corpse-white. "Maybe it's your job to keep people persuaded! Could be that's what you're doing here."

Eric laughed.

"Think it's funny, Eric? You gonna tell me those planes weren't part of a U.S. government conspiracy? Invented in every detail?" He raised his voice. "And fuck the people! A monster conspiracy, right?"

Eric looked into Taylor's small, very blue eyes with an expression of serious sympathy.

"That's precisely what I am telling you, Taylor."

"The phone calls! The whole thing invented by baby-raping motherfuckers. And you, man — who we don't want in this house — I can tell you're one of them!" He breathed heavily. "Second plane! Third plane! Bullshit!" he shouted.

Annie knew the one thing she could not do was threaten to leave the room or actually leave it. To her surprise and dread, Eric seemed oblivious to the danger. He laughed into Taylor's uncomprehending rage, his eyes wild. He looked desperate until his gaze settled on the fire.

"It's all conspiracy," he said to the fire, then looked to Annie. "It's all conspiracy, Annie. I can explain it for you."

Neither of them answered him. Annie wondered briefly if she might hear some valuable information. She thought it unlikely.

"You guys heard about history being mere fiction? That's the way it's always been. Heard of the Romans?" Eric demanded. "They never existed!" He raised his voice. "It's baloney. I mean there's Rome, right. But there never were any Romans with togas and shit, and helmets and feathers. A fairy tale out of the Vatican Library. They even dreamed up the idea of a Vatican Library. There isn't one!"

Taylor and Annie exchanged looks.

"The Greeks! There weren't any Greeks, not ever. I know there are Greeks, but they're not *the* Greeks. I've been to so-called Greece. Plato? Mickey Mouse's dog. Babylonians. Israelites? The pyramids are like forty, fifty years old, Annie. Right, Taylor? This shit is all made up by the government. Once more unto the breach, dear friends — what a laugh. You think people in iron suits rode around on horses? Horse *shit* is more like it. Don't give up the ship? I mean — come on!"

Annie became giddily curious to hear what he might say next. It was a kind of intoxication.

"Why?" she asked Eric. "Why do they do it?"

Taylor watched him with what Annie knew to be a gossamer web of caution he might cast off in a moment.

"Why?" Eric shouted. "Why do they do it? To fuck up you and Taylor!" He rose from the table and staggered toward their sofa, half paralyzed with mirth. "You're on all the lists!"

When Eric lay unconscious, Annie half dragged her husband into their bedroom. "You stop where you are!" Annie told Taylor when she had him behind the closed door. "He's passed out and I'm not going to let you kill him in my living room. Forget about it."

"The prick is still laughing," her husband protested.

Annie opened the door a crack and peeked out at Eric, who remained unconscious on their sofa.

"He's dead to the world! Let him be. He'll be gone tomorrow."

Assured of her control, she leaned against him.

"Come, baby. Come on to bed, sweethome."

She got under the handsome white-and-yellow sunburst quilt her friend Vera Gold had done in Boston. Taylor sat down on the bed and slowly undressed. But in a moment he was on his feet again, raging. She knew, however, that it was unlike Taylor to attack in his underwear. He was physically quite modest. When he was settled beside her she took up her night's reading, which involved the captivity narrative of Mary Rowlandson.

"What does he mean, 'the lists'?" Taylor asked.

"Honey? Do you not see that he's a crazy? He's sort of a homeless person, I think."

"I think maybe we should call Lou. Find out if he really knows her."

"Taylor," Annie said, "if anyone would come up with such a guy, it would be Lou."

"I don't like it, Annie," Taylor said. "That conference happens. Then this jerkoff turns up. Then he says we're 'on the lists.'"

"Taylor, everything is not connected. Shit happens, right?" Annie was not sure this was the explanation for it all. It would have to do.

In the morning, somewhat to their astonishment, Eric and his bag had vanished. Their dinner table was clean and scrubbed, the dishes all washed and stacked. Eric had left a daisy and a wild rose on the table, and a note with them that read:

"Daisies are better than meat, and roses are sweeter than wine."

"Fuck's that mean?" Taylor asked her.

When she went outside the fog was still heavy on the island. As she drove Taylor to the ferry slip they passed Eric slogging unhappily downhill.

"It's him!" Taylor said, craning his neck to look.

"Yup." Annie said.

"Well, at least you didn't stop to give him a ride."

"At least he's not riding a black helicopter," said Annie.

At the ferry slip armed men in flak jackets who looked as though they actually belonged in black helicopters had more or less barricaded the dock.

"You're late for school," Taylor told his wife as he put his ID card around his neck. "Better rush."

"I'm late anyway." She watched Taylor hold up his papers in a surly way for the agents. They looked after him briefly as he walked up the gangway.

Annie drove back through town and up the hill toward home. On the way she passed Eric making slow progress down. She made a two-point turn and pulled up beside him.

"C'mon, Eric," she said. "I'll give you a ride as far as town." Eric threw his bag in the back and climbed into the passenger seat.

"Do you remember us?" she asked him. "Taylor and me?"

"I remember you."

"Thanks for the daisy," she said. "Hey, you're the height of weirdness."

"Right."

"You were living dangerously last night."

"Yeah. I blunder into that." As they rounded a bluff over the ocean, going slowly in the bad visibility, Eric said, "I fell in love with you. You're beautiful."

She laughed.

"But really," Eric said. He seemed close to tears. "I love you, Annie."

"Yeah? You're funny. Last night you were a scream."

"Didn't you feel it?"

"I'll take you as far as town," Annie said. "Don't forget your bag."

"But didn't you?"

"I'm attracted to you," she said. "That's true."

He raised his hand to his forehead. "So?"

"So nothing," she said.

On Heron's Neck that morning the Secretary was cross. When the steward came knocking he swore at the man.

"Aye aye, sir," the steward said soothingly through the door. Of course they were Navy stewards and that was naval usage, but it was not a phrase often heard outside the uniformed branch. Then, from a distant corridor, what sounded like a disrespectful utterance echoed for a second or two. Some barbarous holler, maybe in Tagalog. It was strange and it made the Secretary angry. Certain arms of the naval intelligence service believed an Austronesian-speaking spy agency was providing Moro jihadis with information on naval operations. It was similar to the Mormon yeoman spies the Joint Chiefs had run in the Nixon days and to the Mossad frames that functioned with American collaborators under several Israeli governments.

The fog was thicker than ever. There was a breeze spinning the mist but it seemed not to help, and the settled damp looked dirty to the Secretary. No poetry in this soiled cotton blanket. The Secretary actually wrote poetry. One poem began:

> *If I manifest manhood's pride*
> *Yet I know its pain, its secret*
> *Griefs . . .*

Not much poetry in anything that day, though. And he had the odd feeling that the night before, his six-month plan had been brushed aside politely. Better, he thought, to have kept his mouth shut and waited for signals.

There seemed no question of flight this Monday. Coast Guard cutters prowled the fog for foolhardy windsurfers, lost sport fisherman, disoriented boaters. The Navy's small boats were one cape away. The Secretary ordered that the ferry be chartered again. His security detail drove him to the pier.

"I guess it didn't occur to you to provide for this," he said to the chief of his detail as they drove over the moor. Depressing dark green vegetation, what you could see of it.

"Sir" was all the agent said. A swarthy man, short hair treated at the top in some contemporary fashion. The Secretary looked at him long enough for his stare to register. "I suppose that's not your job." The damn automated foghorn kept sounding its cadences as it had in and out of his anxious dreams.

"Transport confirmed at the seat of government, Mr. Secretary."

A gruff military type, the Secretary thought. More gruff than ought to be allowed. The Secretary wanted some explication of the agent's jargon but thought better of it. He knew enough to recognize it as an unfavorable portent. Everyone seemed ill-tempered, even people who had no right to be.

On Heron's Neck, the Secretary had spent an uneasy night, though not for want of medication. He had lain awake a long time, and just when he began to drop off, a steward rapped quietly but insistently at his door. The steward knocked quietly out of discretion, but also because, awakened suddenly, the Secretary sometimes shouted. Even *screamed*, the stewards told each other, and the word passed into use from the Secretary's households into government and political circles. A woman he happened to know who had called him owlish had also referred to him as Screamin' Newton. Someone had managed to let him know this, a false friend, a subordinate who had not been well-intentioned toward either of them. The word was that the pressures were getting to him.

While the Secretary waited in his vehicle on the dock, his security detail's chief and Captain Negus of the MV *Squanto* were having a bad-tempered, pointless exchange over the gangway's having been down all night. The chief of security had angered Negus by insisting the captain had been ordered to secure it.

"Wasn't by you," Captain Negus said.

"No, it wasn't by me, Ace. Personally, not by me. But you were ordered to keep the vessel secure with the gangway up. That didn't get done, did it? So guess what?"

Captain Negus did not like to be dressed down by people in sunglasses, which, off season, he took as a sign of moral inauthenticity. He was a buoyant soul, pretty easygoing but not used to scoldings. When the local Coasties checked his underway on-board passenger numbers or the supply of children's life jackets, the atmosphere was not chummy, but it was respectful, and there were handshakes without snipe or snip or snot like with the goddamned Heron's Necks. Captain Negus did not like being asked to "guess what?" because it brought to mind his unhappy childhood. Least of all did he like being addressed by a younger man as Ace. Captain Negus was proud of his past military time, although he shared several attitudes with Taylor Shumway, who was after all his second cousin.

"You'll have to tell me, mister. I ain't much of a guesser."

What the gruff agent delighted in telling him was that the boat would have to be gone over completely again, big spaces and small spaces, because the enemy's devices came in all shapes and sizes. His crew would have to have their papers checked again. It would take a lot of goddamn time and the Secretary would have to wait and the scheduled customers would have to take the ferry after his. When they walked out from under the car deck, the rain was falling harder and the security detail had put on their lettered rainwear and were reading the crewmen's laminated IDs again. A Coast Guard engineman, a boatswain's mate and one of the detail went through the vessel's spaces for the second time.

After the security detail finished with the captain and crew and allowed them behind the auto barrier, the Secretary got out of his car and began measuredly pacing the plank section of the pier. He was so angry that he found it necessary to imagine subordinates, inadequate ones, close by. It was better than feeling alone. Sometimes, alone in silence, he would imagine dialectical conflicts with enemies, turning their taunts against them, making them out to be utter fools. Of course they were imaginary. Two agents monitored the ovoid orbit of his pacing.

The rain eased again. Soon segments of blue appeared overhead. "What do they pay these weather dudes?" someone in the waiting group asked. "They should stick to balloons or drones," someone else said, and a third person muttered under her breath. But they did not seem to be changing arrangements. The Secretary continued his rotations.

When it became plain to the small civilian crowd that no one would share the Secretary's boat in any weather, folks began sauntering away. Some strolled toward the pretty town, some to see if they could reclaim Heron's Neck.

Captain Negus and Taylor Shumway stood on the A deck, one up from the car deck, looking at the scene. Scully, a boozy but efficient deck sailor from away, stood beside Jimmy Slaughter, the dockmaster, who was very short and fat. Jimmy never went to the mainland, and for that reason never bothered about his few yellow teeth, which were mostly lower incisors. His appearance annoyed the senior menials at Heron's Neck, which cheered him somewhat. Jimmy had two assistants, his children. One was Jin, the pretty blonde in the Bosox cap on the dock. The other was Jimmy Slaughter Junior, a youth with his father's shape but with fresher tattoos and the island's first, only, and apparently last Mohawk. Both male Slaughters had been impressed for the trip across.

"Son of a bitch tells me I ain't allowed onto my own goddamn boat all night," Captain Negus said.

"Lookit the Secretary or whatever," Scully said. "Fuckface dimwit. Turkey."

"Jeez," Jimmy Slaughter said, "gimme a passenger load of drunks anytime over these weasels." He shook his head at them, causing one security agent to frown from the dock.

"Yah, well," Jimmy's cocky son told his father. "Good money for this, right?"

"Ya," the captain said, "you get a receipt but ya gotta wait for it. Your fuckin' fuel's twice as much by then. Taxpayers don't get it. Never will. Fuckin' nation of sheep."

"'He calleth his own sheep by name,'" Taylor said rather bitterly.

"So? That there's in the Bible or what?" Scully asked. But Taylor was too amazed and upset to answer. He had recognized a man on the dock as his recent guest, Eric. He began to tremble.

Some of the disappointed passengers and their friends were being accosted by Eric with a notebook. They appeared to appraise him as a nobody at best. Eric also approached some of the politicians, who with their wives graciously eased around him with sour looks. One politician wished him a pleasant morning. Another actually said that it was good to see him again. But it became obvious to the Secretary's detail, if not to the Secretary himself, that Eric's spindle-legged progress was directed toward that official.

Scully was trying to engage Taylor for reassurance. The kid had his fits, not that he couldn't work right through them. No one could say he wasn't a good worker. Scully was also trying to engage Captain Negus's eye.

"Know what?" Scully said. "Now they took Johnny Damon down there and made him look like a fuckin' salesman." By "down there" Scully meant New York or Washington or anywhere. Scully called Cape Ann "down there" and the Bay of Fundy "down there."

"You're right," Taylor said, but he never lost sight of Eric. His thoughts were confused but his anger was not in the least diminished. "I'll be a son of a bitch," he said. No one responded to this.

Scully went on about Johnny Damon.

"Fuckin' Steinbrenner," he cawed. "Says he looks good now, he looks like a Yankee." He noticed Taylor's evil eye on the pier. "I kinda liked it when Johnny Damon looked sort of like you, Taylor."

Below them, the Secretary was screaming at Eric. Eric was trying to smile. But the Secretary simply kept screaming, halting some of the in-crowd — though only for a moment — in their tracks.

"Look at the little rat," the Secretary screamed. The chief of security put his weight against the Secretary as if assisting him to stand. He might also have seemed to be holding him back. Ignoring the Secretary, two other agents, one male, one female, were taking Eric down.

"Why are they doing that to him?" Taylor asked.

"They better do that on town property," said Negus. "I don't want that crap on the *Squanto*. A passenger got certain rights."

"Stay down, sir," said the female agent as the Secretary carried on. They succeeded in leveling Eric to the wet pavement. Other agents came over quietly. The one in closest custody of Eric was a black woman in a gray pantsuit.

"I wanted to especially ask you," he told the woman. "I hoped we could talk."

"You lucked out." She lifted Eric's leg as though she were about to make a wish on him while her colleagues kept him prone. She ran cupped hands up the khaki pants, ripped out the cuffs where they had been sewed and twisted Eric's leg to rotate it on the hipbone, each twist eliciting a groan. Then she let the leg fall.

"When's the last time you ate, sir?" she asked him. Eric mistook her question for solicitude, but it was just profiling.

"Christ," Taylor asked no one special, "isn't he one of them or what?"

"Shit," said Jimmy Slaughter Senior, "you fuckin' got me. Don't seem they like him a lot."

The town constable's patrol car, which had been idling behind a taffy stand, rolled out to receive Eric. The chief security agent, the one Captain Negus particularly disliked, was trying to make himself heard in the pilothouse, turning colors, dancing, silently singing, waving his hands alternately in menace, supplication, inviting harmonies. He wanted the captain to get the boat under way. The Coast Guard had driven their Secretary, invincible within the vehicle, thirty feet onto the car deck. The security agent refused to stop capering below the wheelhouse.

Negus buried it all under the sounding of his vessel's horn. He hardly looked down at the agent, who was half kneeling, holding his ears.

On the pier Eric was smiling dementedly.

"Well I'll be goddamned," Taylor said. "That dipstick thought it was a joke."

"He was over your house last night, I heard," Jimmy Slaughter said.

Taylor grunted.

As they pulled away from the pier, Officer Ussolini, the constable, drove Eric slowly up the hill in his squad car. "I thought he was one of them," Taylor told Scully. They were swabbing an interior passage that had been soiled by the authorities' unnecessary second inspection.

"They're all one of them," Scully said. "Eat from the same trough. Fuck their little differences, they ain't no friends of mine." He paused and leaned over his swab. "You all right, kid?"

Taylor kept swabbing, trying to dig the mop deeper into the steel deck than was possible or the work called for. When he had worn himself down he stepped out through the hatch onto the ladder that led to the wheelhouse and looked out over the ocean. There was a fair wind up, the sky clearing fast. Scully spotted Taylor in his half reverie and winked at Jimmy Junior three ladder steps above them. Taylor was in deep-think mode.

"Guy was okay," he said quietly to Jimmy Junior, "once he stopped drinking and trying to grow weed out west."

In his reverie Taylor was pondering Eric. Just a nihil-ist. Nihilists, Taylor believed, were the living dead. They couldn't take a punch and you couldn't wake them up with one. Whatever made them the way they were made them allergic to light, so they lived their lives outside it, laughing down holes. No wonder this Eric had transformed himself into the world's biggest asshole. Wasn't even his fault. And that was why he was so ugly and stupid and clammy and walked and talked and drank and mocked like a fool. Dead to grace. All of it suspended, withdrawn, none within, none without. But, he thought, Annie was wicked smart and you needed to pay attention to her at times. She had done well, Taylor considered, to spare Eric the beating of his life.

"Look at that bastard," Scully said to Taylor. "Looks like a fat turkey, don't he?"

"That's about it," Taylor said. His attention turned to the Secretary, who was walking to lean on the car deck's rail. You can't teach a man like that through mercy, Taylor thought. Born to kill — kill the grass they walk on and their own kind. Then you got a lot of them never knew a god-damn thing except what some flunky told them that they wanted to hear and they never so much as thought about it again.

Scully and Taylor looked off to starboard and saw an old swordfishing boat, all lines and shrouds and pulpit, running toward the ferry harbor. The fog was clearing as fast as your eyes could handle it.

"Holy shit," said Scully. "How long since you saw one of them? There ain't even any more swordfish."

"Sportfishing," Taylor explained. "Too much time and money. Now, the old man" — he meant Negus — "could tell you how they ran thirty, thirty-five of them sweethearts from Block Island Sound to Nova Scotia. Right outa this harbor."

The Secretary stood against the rail of the car deck be-tween two worried-looking agents, the Afro-American woman and a younger man. The agents' concern did not seem to center on the Secretary in any personal way, but to involve the things around them, spare, uncomplicated things that seemed to menace them — the ocean, the clear-ing sky, car vibration from the ferry's engines.

"I need more air," the Secretary told his guardians. None of the three looked at the others.

"Where would you be comfortable, sir?" one of the agents asked.

The Secretary looked up the ladder toward the next deck. Taylor and Scully were working just above that one, right below the wheelhouse.

"Would you like to sit on a bench outside, sir?" the young man asked. "There's a row of benches topside."

"He's speaking to me like I was a geriatric patient," the Secretary complained to the woman. "I'll tell you where I want to go."

The younger agent led the way up to the A deck. The woman climbed behind. Jimmy Slaughter Junior popped his head out of the hatch to have a look.

"You people have to be there?" the young agent called up. Captain Negus heard him on the bridge, looked down through the glass and swore at him.

"No," he muttered, "we'll just let you shitbirds drift over to Portugal."

The Secretary took a seat at the end of the row of outside benches. This left the young male agent with no place to sit, so he manfully placed his hands on the backing of the seat row and stood to the Secretary's right. The young woman stood behind them.

The Secretary turned his head to fix the agents with his raptor's eye.

"Sometimes," he said, "I wonder if I get the best of you people."

The woman in the pantsuit flushed under her dark skin.

"Sir, the presidential detail . . ." she began. Her colleague was violently shaking his head to caution her. From farther down the A deck the chief agent was walking toward them, arms folded.

Then the Secretary leaped to his feet. He pointed up at Taylor.

"You stupid long drink of water," he screamed. "You useless little scut runner. You're staring at me!"

The agents leaped to their feet, but the Secretary was halfway up the metal stairway to the hatch where Taylor was polishing brightwork. Taylor was taken by surprise. The younger agents were coming up fast, the chief agent behind them. The victim of his own astonishment, Scully froze and stared.

"You murdering dog!" Taylor shouted back at the Secretary. "Shittin' up our island while mothers' sons die! You goddamned pirate." Scully backed down the ladder, keeping an eye on them.

"You faggot," the Secretary yelled at Taylor. "Think you push me around? You measly punk." The agents struggled with him in vain. He commanded the strength of madness.

Taylor's recollection of the struggle would always be compounded of confusion and a lust to kill. His veins and muscles were engorged for combat, but his arms still trembled. He was so surprised and angry he could not make his hand obey his own strength. Next, to his disbelief, he was airborne, falling and headed straight for the water below.

Captain Negus killed the engines and wheeled to port. Scully was shouting. The whole crew came to the rail one deck down, all of them shouting at once, "Man overboard!" as the young agents looked on. Scully turned on the *Squanto*'s emergency siren and slid down the rails of the inboard ladder. Everyone took off for their man-overboard stations. The two youngest agents, male and female, were in a tangle at the foot of the ladder.

The Secretary raised his arms to heaven, looking wild-eyed and triumphant. Captain Negus's repeated blasts of the ship's horn were confusing to everyone.

The Secretary's face was as bright as Moses' own. Laughter foamed and bubbled in his throat and spilled over his teeth. He had lost his glasses.

"Did you see that? Pathetic punk of a loser. Tried to kill me and got his own skinny ass wasted."

In the water, not as cold as he had feared, Taylor felt himself slipping toward the *Squanto*'s hull. The green-painted freeboard below the fender rose and fell above him like a living wall; she was underloaded and high in the water. With all his strength Taylor set off in a rowing backstroke to put ocean between himself and the hull, the slowing screws aft. Falling, he had sunk deep, but he was quick and at home in the water. The *Squanto* hurried past him as though she were fleeing for the ferry dock. He rested on his back and breathed regularly.

The agents and the crewmen on the *Squanto* tried to carry the Secretary down to the row of seats below.

"Don't move him right now," the chief agent said. "Keep him still."

"Did you see it, you men? Got his own skinny ass wasted."

The Secretary struggled with his bodyguards, attempting to assault Taylor again. The chief agent looked up at Captain Negus.

"Let's get this thing to Quonset Point," he said. "There'll be an ambulance."

"We got a man in the water, officer," Jimmy Slaughter told the agent. "I think we best get him back."

They did not have to put a boat over to get Taylor aboard. Jimmy Junior and Scully guided him back with marlinspikes and hauled him over by force of arms. Scully brought blankets and coffee from the galley. The agents had stayed beside the Secretary, who sat in a swoon of triumph. His screams, celebrating his strength and overcoming, echoed off the metal bulkheads. He declined coffee in order not to be interrupted and even refused a blanket.

Scully and the crew looked on while the agents took Taylor's coffee from his hands and tossed it over the side. Two of them bent his arms behind him and forced him to his knees on the deck. One slid plastic handcuffs over his wrists.

"You're under arrest for assault on an officer of the United States cabinet and on federal officials," the young woman informed him.

Negus, who had sent Jimmy Junior up to take the wheel, interrupted her reading of Taylor's rights.

"Fuck you doin'?" he asked her.

The woman blazed up at him. "You got a problem, sir? You stand aside or you're going with him."

"Listen, Captain," the senior agent said wearily. "Just get this thing to Quonset Point. We got an ambulance and backup there."

Captain Negus looked at his watch.

"We ain't going to Quonset Point," he told the agent. "Ace! Officer! Quonset Point's over two hours aboard this motor vessel. I got a crewman freezing cold and maybe injured. I'm going to the island Coast Guard station."

"Sir," said the agent in charge, "they don't have what we require there."

"I know what they got there, Ace. They got a chief corpsman. The victim got a wife there."

"The victim?" the agent in charge asked.

The young woman stood as if transfixed. She spoke rapidly and mechanically.

"We'd have to get a helicopter for the Secretary's safety," she declared. "We can't take the perpetrator in the same aircraft or vehicle. I haven't read this man his rights!" she said, turning toward Taylor as though he were unoccupied space. "I haven't finished reading the subject his rights."

"I know my rights!" Taylor shouted. Scully came out of the galley with another cup of coffee for him and a replacement blanket. In an after hatchway, the Secretary was locked in silent struggle with a much larger agent, and the others turned to watch him. After a moment the big man prevailed and drew the Secretary out of the hatchway.

"I seen it," Scully told them all. "Kid just passed a remark. Crazy old fuck threw him over."

"We all saw it," the captain said, although he had not, really. "Kid just passed a remark."

When they tied up, the Secretary was free of restraint though closely observed by his guardians. The crewmen were telling the agent in charge that they had all seen it. Taylor had simply passed a remark. The agent in charge seemed to be writing it down. On the dock, people took pictures of the Secretary's triumphant turn around the top deck. He was smiling broadly. But suddenly his mood changed. He began to snarl and swear at the small crowd.

"Sir," one of the agents asked the cabinet officer, "would you like to come down and take it easy?"

"Like hell," said the Secretary. "Feeling fine. I'm not

afraid — we have to defend ourself from fanatics. Little bastard!" he screamed. "Scum of the earth! Ha ha!"

Officer Ussolini took Captain Negus's report over the satellite phone. He pulled up in his squad car, lights flashing. Negus went down to the pier to talk to him.

"What's the matter with him?" the island cop asked. "He go nuts or something?"

"Nuts? He thrown Taylor Shumway off the ferry."

Ussolini stared at him.

"So?" he asked after a minute. "Is there a complaint?"

"I got a complaint. I don't know about America in general."

"You mean he just tossed Taylor over? Without no provocation."

"Wasn't any. Old guy's bad-eyeing Taylor. Kept him from work. Interfered with him. You know Taylor. He passed a remark."

"Jeez."

"Next thing the guy puts Taylor in the drink. No provocation, not particularly, no. His own detail tried to stop him."

"This is a high-ranking individual," Ussolini said.

"Christ," the captain said, "that's the whole point, ain't it?"

While they talked, one of the agents walked over to the squad car.

"We'd appreciate it if this incident was kept confidential," the man told them.

"Yeah, what am I supposed to tell the company? What do I tell the Coasties?"

The agent was annoyed. "We'll take care of that, boss. Don't worry about it."

"Lot of people seen it," Negus said.

"Don't take it on yourself — you know what I'm saying?"

On the top deck of the ferry, the Secretary seemed to be in flight from his own security detail. The chief agent looked around uncomfortably. His eye fell on Eric, who looked disheveled and was walking up to the pier.

"Who's that guy? Didn't you have him in custody?"

"We're not holding him. He's just some writer," Ussolini said.

Approaching the gangplank now, the Secretary seemed to be edging away from his guards, who were moving subtly to block his path.

Negus and the officer watched Eric. He was looking for his glasses, which were hanging from his shirt collar.

"He's a freelance reporter. He's on assignment for *Roxy* magazine."

"*Roxy*?" Negus asked. "I thought they were a fuckbook."

"That's what I thought. But I talked to this woman editor — sounded educated. Like she had clothes on."

"What do you know!"

"I called Sheila, too, to come down." Sheila Toolin was the all-season doctor on the island. "And you know what? They said forget about it. They got their own doctor."

"Keepin' quiet about it, ain't they?"

"I hope someone told Annie."

"I told her," the cop said, shaking his head. "Bells of hell, Delbert, you didn't want to be there for that." Ussolini looked up the hill. "She'll be coming down with Sheila.

They better get the old fucker off island. Anyway, I bet ya Annie gets it in the paper next week. Me, I gotta write a report. Them Secret Service, they'll be scattered to the winds of the world. I gotta live here."

"I wonder how much of a screwball old Eric over there is. Hey, Eric!" Negus beckoned Eric with the crook of a finger. "You do stuff off the record?"

"Of course," Eric said. "I never got anyone in trouble for talking to me." This was not altogether true. Eric could be quite discreet, however. "Did the Sec really throw Taylor off the boat?"

Officer Ussolini looked troubled.

"Wait a second, Del," he said.

"Word's gettin' out, Charlie," Captain Negus told the policeman. "Annie's gonna write about it. You're gonna write it up for the record. They know they can't kill it."

"Yeah," Ussolini said. "But Eric's — pardon me, Eric — he's a little strange."

"No, no," Eric said. "I only appear strange. You can check my clips. My background."

The two of them watched him. "I could call you," Eric suggested, "'officials familiar with the circumstances.' I wouldn't have to say 'local officials' if you didn't want me to. If the Coast Guard investigated, I could say 'Homeland Security officials.'"

"They couldn't kill it after that, could they, Charlie?"

"Trust me," Eric said. He gave the captain his card. "I'll be in touch."

Being led tenderly up the gangway, the Secretary was sure he spotted wise guys in the crowd. Some were taking photographs with their cell phones. Agents advanced on them threateningly. A reporter on the dock was wrestling an agent for his laptop.

"How do you like it now, gentlemen?" the Secretary called merrily to the people on the dock. That, he happened to know, was what Hemingway used to say to wise guys.

In a day or so, Eric sneaked back onto the island to interview his eyewitnesses. Taylor refused to speak to him. Annie also refused. But in the end it was Annie, working day and night at the island paper, who got her version of the events in print before anyone else. Annie's version was extremely partisan but convincing enough for the paper's owner to triple the print run and sell copies on the mainland. Blogs picked it up before the mainstream press did, together with YouTube videos of the Secretary's tantrum. The package was a great success.

A magistrate dismissed the charges against Taylor on the grounds that he had only passed a remark. The Sorenson-Shumways were not litigious and sought no settlement, although they were irritated to discover that in common law the king could do no wrong.

The public relations people at Defense were unable to keep the story under control. The plenitude of YouTube scenes provided evidence more vivid than any description of Annie's or Eric's ever could. In them, the Secretary railed against the CIA and its collaborators, who were mainly Filipino Mormons from Panay, paid handsomely to spy on him.

His mission completed, Eric left the island forever and never saw Annie or Taylor again. Six months later in India he was reunited with Lou, who explained ectomorphism and its relationship to alcoholism and mayhem. Eric and Lou went to Bali together, and then Eric went back to Possibilities.

The Secretary resigned his cabinet post and returned to private life, working on his poetry and translations. Presently he was reported ill, resting at a naval facility near Baltimore. The facility was a twenty-story wedge of brick, almost winged in shape, red brick wings folded each over the other. It seemed capable of some kind of ungainly sudden flight that would appall and unsettle witnesses. Its wings hovered over a courtyard a hundred feet below. The Secretary's accommodations had an exhilarating view of the sky too.

The Secretary's special labor in the months following his embarrassing exposure to the press had been translation. He had been working on little reading costumes calculated to charm an audience, making crowns, transliterating the Greek alphabet. He had fashioned a pillowcase with an eye torn in it for his poem about Cyclops, Poseidon's son:

> Blinkered child of sea and sky
> Made weak by the sly man's trickery,
> Conniving Odysseus laughs and chooses,
> Leaves to you the cursed, the defense of island realm,
>   resounding cavern.
> Defending your island, your realms your caverns
>   resounding.

Then one day he took it to their faces, a banner short and sweet, and on it read: APOTETELEMENON! A strange device to the cowards — Mission Accomplished! Yes, strange to this one and that one, cowards and defeatists! Mission Accomplished, or something close, Victory!

"Nobody's killing me now," the Secretary screamed. And raced them to the window again. It was a close-run thing, but he was overtaken and put to bed.

From the Lowlands

....

LEROY TRAVELED EAST into the high country pursued by little sense of sin. He had made a lot of money being no worse than anyone else in the San Francisco Peninsula data business and in his way contributing a lot. He had gone early to Silicon Valley; he had lived with his first wife in a bungalow, a tiny place in the bamboo near the Stanford golf course. She had worked as a keypunch operator for Bank of America, and he was hired by Lockheed as an analyst.

The place he was headed for was high in the Mountain West, a second home so far upstream on a river called Irish Creek that past it the canyon went to ground. The gorge was still two hundred feet from rim to riverbank, but beyond Leroy's it sank from sight and became a descent into the heart of the high desert. Here the mountain sheep had nowhere to go but down to escape danger, and they had learned over generations to leap from the exposed crags when startled, and disappear into the shadows and scattered sunlight of the sunken canyon.

In some ways the house Leroy had built — or caused to be built — reminded him distantly of the bungalow in Menlo Park. It was much larger, to say the least, and it had a swimming pool. But it accorded with an old need that he was not at all ashamed of: being close to the land. It stood at the far end of the only access road, a mile and a half beyond where the paving ended. Approaching his house the track was only surfaced and sealed. Paving, the realtor had sworn to him, would come soon. When he had spent a few weeks in the house he was not sure he required paving, which would mean his road's extension and more development along the canyon.

Decades before, Leroy had happened by a university research center on one of the rare Saturdays when he was free from Lockheed, and had seen some acquaintances from the company playing with computers. They were the old computers of that time, which, people joked, looked like the Dnepropetrovsk hydroelectric dam. His friends were playing a primordial war game, dogfighting with virtual spaceships, blasting each other's entities on the screen. They were whooping and dancing and having enormous fun. Leroy thought it looked like fun too. He was as fun-loving as anyone, though he liked practical jokes most. He loved what had once been called the put-on, in his own definition of it. For example, on his BMW there was a bumper sticker that read: LOST YOUR CAT? CHECK MY TREADS.

His mountain property had two levels, both of them set well back from the river so he could assure himself that he was not like the reckless householders downstream. Some of them had balanced themselves on picturesque but heart-stopping outcrops, where they could crawl to the edge of their decks and look down over the rim into swirling white water. Leroy never failed to see, in his imagination, their terrifying fall into the canyon, houses and Franklin stoves and heritage tomatoes and trophy wives in a fatal descending whirl.

Leroy and one of his friends from the company were among the young men who employed the principles of the early computer game to establish their electronics company. They called it "electronics" at first, but it became ever so much more. He and the friend, whom he called Dongo, prospered. Life on the San Francisco Peninsula was good; he and Dongo could smoke dope and pick up chicks at Kepler's and party. Everyone had a beard and grew their hair long; it was a statement. You could laugh at the nine-to-five dorks from IBM with their white shirts and scabby close shaves. They laughed back, but not for long when their scene looked like it was going under. Then he and Dongo would sing a song about the IBM types that went:

> *They're drowning in the lowland, low land low,*
> *They're drowning in the lowland sea.*

It had been a long time since those days, but every once in a while the song came back to Leroy. As the drive to his house took him over the high prairie, the sweet land smelling of sage and pine, the plain disappeared into a dizzying impossible perspective that ended where the white-clouded, snowy, sawtooth-shaped peaks rose. Approaching the head of the valley, he hummed and sang "drowning in the low-land sea," not really thinking of IBM or Dongo or the First Girl or anything much. Just sort of singing along with the tumbling tumbleweed.

Dongo had really liked to party. Too much party, old Dongo. Dongo had turned Leroy on to acid once — there had been a lot around then — but Leroy, with his enthusiasm for work and his strong business sense, had not gone near it ever again. In fact, watching Dongo had led him to stop using dope altogether. Moreover, he had found a chick, not that he would call her a chick anymore. A woman, a woman who taught him all of love that he would ever know, which on the emotional level was not really too much. Barbara, the most beautiful of all things California.

Then Dongo starting losing it. Really. Dongo got so into acid that he thought he could teleport himself to remote galaxies. Much as Leroy loved the land, Dongo went utterly insane over the idea of it and moved to the toolies of Humboldt County. Leroy had been forced to take what was called in Communist dictatorships of the time "strong measures," as his Romanian girlfriend Ilena liked to say. Ilena's mother had been a commissar. Leroy had been forced to cut poor Dongo loose. He was able, legally it turned out, to take over the business, a fair-means-or-foul sort of thing, a dire necessity. One way or another.

Times were not then tough, but there was no knowing. Dongo was beyond help. Leroy never knew quite why he called Paul Dongo. There was just something Dongo-like about the guy. Poor Dongo hadn't liked it much from the first day, although he had never said "Don't call me Dongo." Probably, Leroy thought, he sensed where the power was.

The petty resentment actually helped when the time came to move on, and Leroy, as anyone would, did what he had to do. What happened then was Barbara the beautiful, on some kind of fucking cosmic ray, beamed herself to Dongo up in Dongoville, California, but she came crawling back after a year and Leroy unwisely married her. Dongo died — had to happen. Leroy's marriage was brief.

Halfway across the prairie below Leroy's house was the Salikan River, of which his Irish Creek was a fork, and along the Salikan was an old mining town with the same name. Half the town's houses were post-sixties, alpine style or Old Westy, but there were fifties ranch houses, a steepled Mormon church and a black-and-white-movie motel at the top of the bluff over the river. An old general store stood beside it that had an *Oakland Tribune* newspaper rack on the wood sidewalk outside, though Oakland was nearly a thousand miles away, and insofar as Leroy could remember there was no such paper. Leroy parked his BMW out front.

The newspaper rack was always empty because Beck, the proprietor, was afraid that people would take newspapers without paying. Leroy himself had made a practice of doing that. Still, he wondered about Beck's savage irascibility. People around Salikan called Beck Caw or Crow or Craw or something of the sort, some sound they made. Craw was an older gentleman, as the wry youth of California said, God knew how old. There was a woman who worked with Craw sometimes, and Leroy had taken to thinking of her as Slob, which was his name for poorly groomed, overweight individuals. Slob, he presumed, was Craw's daughter, but who knew the relationships between these people?

Leroy straightened up as he stepped onto the wood sidewalk. Maybe it was the influence of westerns: something about shed-like buildings with wooden sidewalks made a man feel like walking tall. And Leroy was in good shape. He worked out regularly. He thought it made him stand out from the obese jerkarounds you saw in town and at the downscale mall in the valley. The little bell tinkled when he opened the door of Beck's store. Craw and Slob were both behind the counter.

"Afternoon, folks," Leroy said going in.

Old Craw looked at his watch. Slob gave him a soft hello.

"Hey, Beck," Leroy asked, "you got the *Oakland Tribune*?" Leroy thought he might have made that joke before. Old Beck never looked at him. The daughter answered.

"Hasn't been an *Oakland Tribune* for a great many years," she said. "I'm surprised you ever heard of it, your age."

Leroy was pleased. Indeed, he appeared considerably younger than his years.

"I haven't," he told her, and walked away. He heard the old man start to say something but get shushed by his daughter.

Strolling down to the dairy case to get some skim milk, he was reminded of the first heavyset person he referred to as Slob. He was good at nicknames, at least he thought so, and pretty original. Some people, he thought, practically named themselves by not caring how they looked. The other Slob was a young man who had worked for Leroy, a bit of a genius type, too much so. Leroy had started out calling him George. Slob the First became political and made objectionable noises about contracts with the Defense Department. Some systems went into the making of cool modes of

weaponry that featured nasty surprises for enemy person-
nel and their dependents. Of course they did terrible things
to people — they were weapons, for Christ's sake. As much
as anything else they reminded Leroy of the computer war
games at the research institute. But it was the age of the agi-
tator; people needed to piss and moan. If Slob First had not
been so obnoxious about it, Leroy would not have conceived
the plan to make him disappear, corporately speaking.

While Leroy was fetching his quart of milk and dozen
eggs, a bunch of drive-through tourists came in. The man
was slight and overpolite to Craw and Slob behind the counter, tentative and ingratiating as your drive-through tourists
tended to be. His wife acted the same way, smiley, hi there.
The wife was a babe in nice-fitting jeans and a tight University of Wisconsin, Milwaukee, T-shirt with a blue hoodie
over her hair. They had a child of about five, who unfortunately for the kid resembled his dad. While the couple fid-
dled around the counter, the lad wandered down the rows
toward the dairy section where Leroy was getting his milk
and eggs.

The little boy looked about him blankly. Leroy had a sudden impulse. Craw kept the candy under his birdy eye at the
counter but his supply boxes were in the back, near where
Leroy was standing. One carton of expensive chocolate bars
stood beyond the child's reach but available to Leroy's. He
reached up and took a bar of imported chocolate out. Catching the child's eye, he made a small clicking sound of conspiracy and handed it to him. After a moment the child took
it and put it in his pocket.

At the counter Leroy paid a simmering Craw Beck for his

purchases. Seven dollars, no less. The family group was at the counter behind him. Before Leroy reached the door, Craw exploded.

"You plan on paying for the boy's candy?"

He was speaking not to Leroy but to the father of the little boy.

"What candy?" the man asked.

"The candy in his pocket!" Craw said with a vicious smile. Beside him, Slob frowned. The wrapper was in plain view.

"He's not even allowed to eat candy!" the father said. More surprised, Leroy thought, than angry. A mild type. Leroy had paused with one hand on the door, a disinterested onlooker.

Turning to look at Leroy, the woman recalled what she had told herself she could not possibly have seen in the space of a moment. She gasped and pointed at him.

"That man!" she said. "He gave it to Todd. I'm sure he did."

Leroy shrugged. Slob looked at him suspiciously.

"Well, damn well put it back or somebody pay for it," said Craw.

Leroy went out at once and put the scene behind him.

Halfway between Beck's store and the post office he encountered a tall woman whom he had nicknamed Grannykins. It was not that she was particularly grandmotherly, only that the plain metal-rimmed glasses she wore lent her long lean face a certain severity. She came under Leroy's scornful definition of older lady; in fact, she was about his age. She was graying but distinctly handsome and had friendly brown eyes. He had first seen her on a horse. She had said hello to him that day, and he had the distinct impression that she was putting moves on him. It was just sad, he thought. She was so much older than any babe he would ever be seen with. Was she serious?

"And how are you today?" she asked, smiling. "I'm Sal," she reminded him. This woman, Leroy knew well enough, was really named Salikan, after the river. The idiotic name dated her pretty well, he thought, and he wondered how she lived with this embarrassment. Salikan, a dog's name. The thought made him grin, which she took as indicating pleasure in her company. He had the strongest impulse to explain to her what was funny, give her a tip about herself. Leroy had been told that Sal's parents had been rich hippies, descended from a Helena molybdenite tycoon. Leroy had never introduced himself, although she had told him her name many times before.

"Hi!" he said. He had to stop when she did.

"How are things with your house?"

"They're good."

"I ride up by your canyon sometimes," she said.

How pathetic, thought Leroy.

"Yeah, I've seen you."

"I don't go up there so much now. I've got wary."

"Right," Leroy said. "You can't be too careful."

Over her shoulder, he saw the flustered-looking tourist family approaching, snuffling little junior, angry mom, subdued loser dad. Sal saw that she had lost Leroy's interest and went away.

"Well, so long," she said. "*You* take care."

As the tourists passed, Leroy went into the post office to

check his mail. Inside, a clerk stood behind the open parcel counter holding a fly swatter. Leroy went past him to the bank of post boxes, opened his and scooped out the useless paper, real estate ads and supermarket flyers. Just then his eye fell on a row of federal WANTED posters on a glass-cased bulletin board beside the street door and he sauntered over to inspect them. One of the fugitives, Leroy observed, was born Alan Ladd. He sometimes used "Bum" as an alias. Hilarious, thought Leroy. In fact, the man's face was a little daunting. The FBI wanted Bum for unlawful flight to avoid prosecution for the crime of murder, committed a few times over on little provocation. At a distance his picture resembled the old cartoon image of a burglar, plug-ugly in the striped shirt and wool cap. But even Leroy could see that there was a man behind the small dead eyes that looked at you over his flute of a nose. The peculiar nose, the lines around his mouth and his round chin made him look like a bad puppet. Pinocchio. The poster said Alan Ladd had worked as a dog trainer; his face was both swinish and prim. Leroy went out, climbed into his BMW and began the drive upriver toward his house.

The huge sky over the valley showed a late-August afternoon light, and even from the car Leroy could savor the deliciousness of the waning day. In the distance a front was gathering, an enormous darkening tower that rose from the mountaintops to an azimuth where innocent blue began. The clouds, bank heaped on bank, spread like an angel army across a quarter of the sky and closed on the near hills. In his own way Leroy was stirred by the drama of it, but he was not in the mood for rain, not on the road up. The fleecy cumuli that had graced the afternoon were giving way before the front; sudden cloud shadows raced over the landscape. The idea of rain, the shadows, caused him a quick confusion of ideas. They were positive: things changed and he thrived. A man who believed in himself was free. The secret was that you could almost make your own weather if you stayed smart and strong. You could sort of make yourself the mysterious force. Leroy thought good things. He shivered.

The road before him climbed in tightening switchbacks, and it was pure pleasure to follow its turns up the slope. Sometimes his heading was the range of shadowed white peaks across the valley, sometimes the field of black volcanic rock that stretched away from the river. To drive such a car and know what you were doing was to own the road.

Climbing, he passed the last few frame ranch gates and then there were no more cattle grids or mailboxes. Driving the last paved half mile, he came to a cleared lot on the canyon side of the road. A house was being built there, a house as big as Leroy's own, as far as he could tell. About a dozen men worked on the construction — carpenters laying and nailing boards on an upper story, roofers, painters applying an undercoat to a completed separate building across the lot. A mobile roller for laying tar and an articulated loader were parked just off the road. Leroy pulled onto the shoulder. The building lot was surrounded by birches bending to a wind he could not feel at first. One moment, walking toward the construction, he was dazzled by sunlight, dazed by the afternoon heat that rose from the bone-dry earth. In the next, he was in the shadow of the imminent storm overhead, grazed by the wind out of the trees. The crewmen were all looking up the valley into the storm that seemed about to break.

Leroy was curious about the house that would be neighboring his. Its rising presence agitated him. On the one hand, he was annoyed that construction upriver was advancing. On the other hand — and he had not thought of it much before — there were times when the loneliness of his location impinged on his satisfaction. He wanted to start a conversation with the men working on the site.

"Hi," he called out. Right then he knew it was going to turn out wrong somehow. "Anything I can do for you guys?"

All of them turned toward him at once. For a long time none of them gave him any answer. He looked at each of them in turn. One of them looked like the man on the poster. It caused him a slight intake of breath. Of course it wasn't the same man, but the brutality of the workman's face shocked him a little. Then it seemed that all of them, the lot, had some weird vocabulary of features in common. It looked as though all they were going to do was stare at him, tight-lipped, hard-eyed. Then the man whose face he had thought most resembled the poster said:

"Yeah. Make us rich."

A deeper silence seemed to fall, so that it was possible to hear the river below.

"I'm trying," Leroy said merrily.

No one laughed, though the hard-faced man to whom he had spoken made his features humorlessly reflect Leroy's attempt at a friendly smile, with a curled lip, a show of teeth and raised eyebrows. Everyone stood in place at his workstation, still and staring. As he turned to walk back to the

car, he heard what he had always dreaded in places like Salikan, a rumble of spitty laughter, low growls and arrested
fricatives trailing his departure. The successful man is re-
sented by the hewers of wood and carriers of water. The
wealthy man of taste and means draws the impotent hatred
of the mob. In some countries, Leroy had heard, such people had a clearer sense of their station in life and conducted
themselves accordingly. Whereas here, he thought, it was
supposed to be all jolly rough-and-tumble, and you couldn't
spit in some peon's face when he tried to be smarter than
you. Leroy had some enraging and frightening memories.
Losers could come right to your house.

The turns were sharper and the incline steeper where
the paving gave way to sealed gravel, but Leroy's car rose
smoothly through it all. When he had put the car snugly in
his garage he let himself inside, into the large kitchen, and
poured himself a glass of pinot grigio. It had been a very tir-
ing drive, and Leroy was working on a headache for which
the wine was not a remedy. His eyes were sore; he thought
he might be due to replace his contacts. He had worked hard
at keeping fit, seeming and feeling younger than his age, but
still he had put in the time. He had not been out for an easy
life, and he had not had one. It occurred to him that no matter how a man postponed it, he ended by progressively set-
tling for less. The thought made him angry.

Leroy's canyon home was the newest and biggest house
on the river. Somebody's had to be. He had definitely come
to feel that a house ought not to be outsized or conspicuous,
and his own place caused him a jot of self-consciousness.
The thing was, it had been like a new toy, and hard for him
in the first flush of ownership not to improve on it and add

features. The pool had been something of an engineering feat, but it was a joy, looking cut into the rock, though it really wasn't, and ingeniously supplied with water at great cost. There was glass on one wall of the den, cantilevered so as not to catch the full force of the wind coming down the canyon but commanding a view of the national forest and wilderness to the north and east. It would have been hard for him to say why, but the dimensions of the place made him feel somehow younger. It proved he belonged to an age group below his calendar years, a Bullshit Walks generation. The right people understood.

Maybe he had figured there would be more people around. In the past they always came to pick his brains, to find out what he could do for them, to listen to his strategies and plans. Girls came for the fun and games, an adventure by the pool, the brightness and glossiness. You always had to be careful with girls, he realized. Girls could go a long way toward making or unmaking your reputation, especially in California. Guys came for access, to prove themselves to him, eager for his blessing on some project. He had taken the Orvis trout-fishing course twice in the hope of excelling on the river. He had become a proficient skier, having learned, one on one, from a top Kraut.

Everybody had to be kept in line. The fact was, Leroy knew, to be too accessible was dangerous. Accessibility aroused the predator. When they call you a nice guy, beware. The nice guy will find his brains on the floor — a proverb from somewhere, some newly competitive nation. Leroy could envision his brains on the floor, gray, bloody, posthumously active, refusing to cease their clamor. He often contemplated with satisfaction the brilliance concentrated within his intellect and will. Sometimes, he knew, it burned with too bright a flame.

He was running a supervisory eye over the road and the garage side of the house when it fell upon an undesirable oddity. Tied to one of the aspens over his driveway — certainly visible from the road — was a twisted length of plastic, the kind of transparent tube in which a newspaper might be delivered on a rainy day. The tube was wet, soiled and blackened like something that had washed up in some filthy city gutter. It was knotted on a high branch of the tree so that part of it floated like a pennant over his turnoff, perhaps a signal pennant. Signaling what? His presence? It was unsettling. It made him imagine piracy, a Jolly Roger.

He moved out of the well-appointed kitchen and sat before his floor-to-ceiling window, watching the stormy night darken the borders of the canyon. The black clouds brought down the night sky, the moon that had been rising; the first stars all disappeared. He took his glass of wine outside to the patio, walked down the stone steps to his pool and switched on the poolside lights and underwater illuminations. The sleekness of the lighting was comforting at first. Then in the blue-tinted light he saw that lapping against the tile of his pool was another soiled piece of plastic like the one in the tree. He felt a wave of disappointment — in things, in the sorry aspect of his rewards, blemishes on good fortune. It seemed like the work of a spoiler, and it frightened him. He looked around him. Somewhere in the sunken canyon behind his house thunder broke and echoed massively; the sound of it felt as though it might shake the house on its stone fortress. A fork of lightning struck rimrock overhead, and whether by reflection or a second strike, it lit the can-

yon below in stunning detail, displaying precisely the color-
ing of each cliff, its cuts, layers and scars, its geological history. Leroy stepped back against the rock wall of his house.
There was a smell of scorched sage and burning pine. The
air was bone-dry, and not so much as a drop of rain fell.

He went back inside, finished his wine and poured another. The drink made him hungry — on the trip up he had
not given any thought to food. All that was in the house un-
frozen were the eggs and milk he had bought at Craw's, a
half stick of butter and an unopened jar of caperberries the
beautiful Ilena had brought him months before. The caperberries were imported from Romania, from a place called
Cluj, which happened to be in Transylvania, where Ilena
herself came from. She had always described herself as Tran-
sylvanian, which meant she might have been Romanian or
Hungarian or descended from Saxon or Slavic settlers. Leroy had never asked her. He required only that she be as
beautiful as she was, and as accommodating. To be seen with
her was to command envy and respect and to display the superior quality of his life. Any fool could see her out in Val-
entino and Cole Haan, and that, Leroy thought, was all they
needed to see.

He opened the berries with difficulty and took out the
butter, milk and eggs. He broke an egg onto the Teflon surface of the frying pan. Looking at the yolk under the kitchen
light, he saw that there was a bright blood spot in the center
of it. This was mildly disturbing to such a perfectionist as
Leroy and he tried to remember what it might signify. Perhaps, he thought, the egg was not fresh. Or the opposite.
He stood reflected in his kitchen window against the black
night outside, seeing his own blank face. A flash of lightning

lit the rock landscape outside, revealing the aspens, the plastic flag at the top of one tree. He sipped his wine, put the pan aside and dialed Ilena's number in San Anselmo.

"Allo, Leroy," Ilena said in her husky voice when she heard who it was. "How may I serve you, my kink?"

"I miss you," Leroy told her. "Why didn't you come with me?"

"Aha. Your punishment, *cheri.*"

"Punishment for what?" He smiled wanly at his reflection. "I've been good."

"Good? Ho ho. A good one."

"No, really. Come up, get a morning plane to Rock City. Get one tonight. I'll get you picked up."

"Naah," she said in a vulgar comic voice. He hated her speaking that way. "Naah," she said. "No fuckink way."

Leroy suspected Ilena might be drunk. She had a drinking problem.

"But why, sweetheart? Don't you love your king?"

"Naah," she said.

"Come on."

"Come on," she mimicked. "*Come on.* Leroy, you're a noodle, eh?"

"Please come."

"Naah."

"I'm opening your caperberries. Thinking of you."

She laughed charmingly. "Don't be so stupid. You make me pissed off."

"If you don't come," Leroy said, "I'll make you sorry."

"Ya? I don't think so. How about: Fuck yourself, dollink."

"Listen," Leroy said, trying to change the subject. "I

broke an egg into the pan to cook your berries. There's a red spot in the yolk. What about that?"

She gave a soft canine yip. "Break other egg."

Leroy reached for a second egg and broke it. It also had a red spot in the yolk.

"A red spot," he told her. "Honestly."

"Yes? No shit? Whoa."

"What?"

"Break next egg. Egg next to it."

Leroy did. There was a red spot. He told her so.

"Somebody playing a joke on you, boss. Like the jokes you like. Put-on, pain-in-the-ass jokes you like."

"I thought you liked my jokes, Ilena."

"Naah."

"You always laugh at them."

"Tell your name for me," she said.

"Oh," he said, trying a laugh. "It's harmless." His nickname for her was Strangepussy. Harmless. But who could have told her?

"I laugh when you put-on somebody else," Ilena said. "You too, when someone hurts. You're cruel motherfucker."

"When did you decide this?"

"Lewis tells me."

Lewis was a business associate of whom Leroy had had enough.

"Lewis! He told you? That nitwit?"

"You think? Screw you! Hey, kink, what looks like? The red spot?"

"It's just red."

"Look like skull, no? Tiny skull."

"I don't see a skull."

"Yes!" she insisted bad-humoredly. "You will see. Ask your other girlfriends. Ask Ludmilla, the gypsy."

"Ludmilla's not a gypsy," Leroy said.

"Fuck she ain't. You cheating *cul*. You get what you deserve. Your money is cursed. Your house. Your dick. Skull in the eggs. You will see."

Leroy cleared his throat. "Please, Ilena."

She cursed in her language and hung up.

Holding his silent phone, he looked out of his dark kitchen window again and saw the face of the fugitive Alan Ladd, the ape's face, the tiny eyes. Smiling. And what to call his mouth? Disapproving. A homicidally disapproving mouth. But it was only a vision, imagination. Alan Ladd, his crushed face, his tiny eyes. Alan Ladd was at the wheel of some murder victim's car, perhaps driving on a transcontinental superhighway, otherwise driving a back road in the woods, prowling. Prowling for victims. Beside Alan Ladd a dog was seated, an exquisitely trained pooch, a mechanical dog actually, its teeth honed and gleaming. Maybe Alan and his dog were seeking out a lonely house in the woods marked by a filthy plastic banner.

But there was nothing in the window. The thought was a worm of the brain. Leroy's phantom, the torment of a too busy man dedicated to his work.

"I can and will make life sweet," Leroy said aloud. As frightening as losers are, he thought, I am more. I have the high ground.

He went into the part of his den that served as a library. Lightning flashed beyond the glass wall, thunder boomed in the rock. There was still no rain. On Leroy's reading table was the two-volume *Oxford English Dictionary*. It stood be-

side Bartlett's *Familiar Quotations*, whose citations he used
to crush underlings. The dictionary came equipped with a
magnifying sheet that could be applied to the page to make
the small print more readily legible. Leroy picked up the
sheet and took it into the kitchen. He had not turned the
stove on, so the eggs sat coldly in their pan, complacently
three-eyed in the light, innocent as unborn Cyclopean
babes. Leroy set his magnifying sheet on the pan's rim.

Yes, he saw. The spots might be skulls. They were elon-
gated, cephalic, with inward curves that might mark cheekbones. The tops were rounded, maybe cranial. There were
two tiny rounded darker marks against the blood red that
might represent eyes, little rectangles that could stand for
teeth. A hollowed snout.

Blood spots, though, not portents, nothing intentional.
Whether random biology or a poisoner's mark, Ilena had
made them appear as they did. Out of secret hatred or jealousy, out of the sheer evil of the weak, which he had seen often enough. As so often with the helpless and self-deluding,
she had turned the strength of the strong against her bet-
ters. The tactic of sly inferiors: to set his mind against itself
in a lonely place. All day, he realized, he had been thinking
negative thoughts. Was it something fated, a test of confidence to be proved, as though there were some superforce
that ruled strength, constantly sorting out the chosen, making them risk their gifts and qualities against the little strategies of the lame? Was there some kind of supernaturalism in
the law of survival?

Leroy decided that it did not matter to him. Even if all
the forces of the eternal loser were able to combine against

his superior mind, people like himself had to prevail. Because morality was functional. To be strong was to be hard, to laugh at punks who never dreamed of taking the first step toward getting what they wanted, who never knew. Never knew except to resent and set petty traps.

Oh, and they hated being called by the names they chose for themselves by virtue of their own absurdity. And their humor was frail; they hated the jokes that required them to act out their foolishness and impotence. They had to live the reality that the elected provided for them. In their sheepy droves they hated Leroy and his like.

Angry, he burst out onto the patio. In his rage he brought his hand down hard on his metal outdoor breakfast table, again and again. While his legato echoed on the wall, he heard a faint but curious sound. Looking up, he saw a dark brown shape. It stayed in place without motion. In a moment, the overhead lights above his pool cast two glowing lights on the lower extension of the thing. What glowed was a pair of bright yellow eyes. It was a cat, coiled, about to spring.

Somehow Leroy managed to leap into the pool. His plunge took him below the surface for a second, and as he fought to clear his vision he made himself hope that he had imagined the thing. But then he saw the panther in the very place he had been standing. It was trembling, regarding him from the far edge of time. Its face was skull-like.

Immediately the big cat moved around to the other side of the pool so that it waited behind him. He turned, treading water, fighting for breath. Floating in the middle of the pool was a large red and green beach ball. He put his arms around it to stay afloat, but it seemed to be drifting toward the side of the pool where the cat waited. Leroy came so close that the cat reached out over the water and, as Leroy watched, a pair of claws the size of kitchen knives shot out from its paw's black pads. The cat growled what sounded to him like a command to despair. Leroy, hanging on to his buoyant toy, saw something dreadful that he recognized in the animal grin and extended fangs. Unrelenting confidence. Dead certainty.

Leroy clung to the merry beach ball. The harder he clung to it, the more it seemed to drift toward the panther's reach. Batted by an almost casual thrust of the cat's claw, the ball began to spin in his slippery embrace. The cat was circling the pool, tense but assured as any mere animal could be, feinting, reversing ground. At play. Leroy began to scream for help. His breath was failing, but on each inhalation he clung harder to the whirling ball.

Overhead the stars had come out, the Milky Way. Leroy thought it might be a trail, a way out. All at once from somewhere in the canyon he heard a voice, one he thought he remembered. He called to it for help with all the breath he could summon until he realized that the voice was singing.

"I'm drowning in the lowland, low land low."

The song was one he knew. It was the voice of Dongo. Dongo singing a song in the canyon.

"Drowning in the lowland sea."

Leroy, spinning with the beach ball, began to sing along.

High Wire

....

I FIRST MET LUCY AT a movie premiere at Grauman's
about midway between the death of Elvis Presley and
the rise of Bill Clinton. Attending was a gesture of support for the director, who happened to be a friend of mine.
The film's distributors had made a halfhearted lurch toward
an old-style Grauman's opening, breaking out a hastily dyed
red carpet. A couple of searchlights swept the murky night
sky over downtown Hollywood. By then these occasions
were exhausted flickers of the past, so there were none of
the much-parodied rituals some of us watched in black-and-
white newsreels at the corner Bijou. No more flashbulbs or
narrators with society lockjaw telling us what the talent was
wearing. Neither simpering interviewers nor doomed starlets walking the walk. The camera flashes and the demented
fans crowding the velvet rope were all memories. Hollywood Boulevard was even rattier then than it is now. The
only people around the marquee that night were frightened-

looking Japanese tourists and bright-eyed street freaks with slack smiles.

The picture was no good. It was the forced sequel to a 1960s hit with a plot cribbed from a John Ford movie of the fifties. It featured two very old actors, revered figures from the time of legend, and the point of it was the old dears' opportunity to recycle their best beloved shtick. The withered couple and their more agile doubles shuffled through outdoor adventures and a heartwarming geriatric romance stapled to some bits of fossil western. Attempts had been made to make it all contemporary with winks and nods and brain-dead ironizing.

The audience consisted mainly of people who were there on assignment, out of politeness, or from fear. There were also members of the moviegoing public, admitted by coupons available through the homes-of-celebrities tours and at the cashier counters of cheap restaurants. Raven-haired Lucy, with her throaty voice and dark-eyed Armenian fire, was in the picture briefly, as an Apache maid. I later learned she was not in the theater to take pleasure in the picture or even in her own performance. She had come in the service of romance, her own, involving an alcoholic, Heathcliffish British actor, the movie's villain.

Heathcliff had made Lucy crazy that night by escorting his handsome and chic wife, suddenly reunited with her husband and relocated from London. It seemed that the sight of them had stricken Lucy physically; when I saw her sitting alone a few seats down from me she was cringing tearfully in the darks and lights from the screen.

My first impulse was to leave her alone in her distress. I

was certainly not impelled to a hypocritical display of concern. But it was one of those bells; I was unattached, still single, due to leave town in a week. Maybe I'd had a drink or smoked a joint before the appalling show. Anyway, I moved one seat toward her.

"Nice scenery," I said.

She looked at me in a flash of the Big Sky Country's exterior daylight, removing her stylish glasses to dab at her tears and sitting upright in her seat.

"Oh, thanks."

Her tone was predictably one of annoyed sarcasm, but I chose not to interpret it as the blowing off she intended. Sometimes you can parse a hasty word in the semidark and I decided not to be discouraged, at least not so quickly. I realized then that she had some connection with the picture on the screen. An actress, a production girl?

In those days, I was confident to the point of arrogance. I assumed I was growing more confident with time. How could I know that the more you knew the more troubled and cautious you became, that introspection cut your speed and endurance? We watched for a while and she shifted in her seat and touched her hair. I interpreted these as favorable portents and moved over to a place one seat away from her. At that distance I recognized her among the film's cast. Scarcely a minute later onscreen, Brion Pritchard, her real-life deceiver, callously gunned down her character, the Apache soubrette. I watched her witness the tearjerky frames of her own death scene. She appeared unmoved, stoical and grim.

"Good job," I said.

Lucy fidgeted, turned to me and spoke in a stage whisper that must have been audible three rows away.

"She sucked!" Lucy declared, distancing herself from the performance and turning such scorn on the hapless young indigen that I winced.

"So let's go," I suggested.

Lucy was reluctant to go, afraid of being spotted by our mutual friend the director, who had also produced the film. She expected to look to him for employment before long. However, she seemed to find being hit on a consolation. It was the first glimpse I had of her exhausting impulsiveness.

We sneaked out in a crouch like two stealthy movie Indians, under cover of a darkness dimly lighted by a day-for-night sequence. The two stars onscreen told each other their sad backstories by a campfire. Their characters had the leisure to chat because Apaches never attacked at night.

Across the street, appropriately, a country-and-western hat band from Kyoto was crooning rural melodies. The two of us jaywalked across Hollywood and into the lobby of the faded hotel where the band was performing. A man in a stained tuxedo — an unwelcoming figure — directed us to a table against one wall. I ordered a Pacifico; Lucy had Pellegrino and a Valium.

"It's Canada," Lucy told me.

"What is?"

"The scenery. In the thing over there."

"The thing? You don't remember what the picture's called?"

"I like repressed it," she said, and gritted her teeth. "Sure I know what it's called. It had different titles postproduction."

"Such as?"

"Unbound. Unleashed. Uncooked."

We introduced ourselves and claimed we had heard of each other. For a while we watched the hat act sing and swing. The lads looked formidable under their tilted sombreros. Their lead singer sang lyrics phonetically, rendering interpretations of "I Can't Stop Loving You," "Walking the Floor Over You" and other favorites. Their audience was scant and boozy. There were a few other bold escapees from the premiere across the street.

"You were a great Apache."

She only shook her head. Plainly, even qualified professional regard would take us nowhere. For some reason I persisted.

"Come on, I was moved. You dying. Featured role."

"Dying is easy," she said. "Ever hear that one?"

I had. It was an old actor's joke about the supposed last words of Boris Thomashevsky, an immortal of the Yiddish stage. Surrounded by weeping admirers seeking to comfort him, he gave them a farewell message. "Dying is easy," said the old man. "Comedy is hard."

"They shot different endings," Lucy explained. "One sad, one happy."

"Really?" It was hard to believe they would perpetrate a sad ending with the two beloveds, which would only have made a fatuous movie even worse. When riding a turkey, I believe, cleave to the saddle horn of tradition. But sad endings were a new thing in those years — the era of the worst movies ever made. Industry supremos who hadn't been on the street unaccompanied for forty years were still trying to locate the next generation of dimwits. So they tried sad endings and dirty words and nude body doubles. There was no more production code; movies were supposed to get serious and adult. Sad endings were as close as most of them could reach.

"So I hear. I wasn't there. I didn't read the endings. Like I had other things on my mind. I didn't see it, did I? We're over here."

"Okay."

"I bet they went with the happy, though." She sneaked a quick look around and bit a half of her second ten-milligram Valium. I told her the happy seemed likely.

"Oh," she said, and she smiled for the first time in our acquaintance. "Tom Loving. You're a writer." She either guessed or had somehow heard of me. Her smile was appropriately sympathetic.

She told me they had reshot a lot during the filming, different versions of different scenes.

"I die in all of them," she said.

Eventually we drove our separate cars to an anchored trailer she was living in on the beach in Malibu. As I remember, she was tooling around in a big Jaguar XJ6. We sat under her wind-tattered awning on the trailer's oceanfront deck and a west wind peeled wisps of cold briny fog off the water. It was refreshing after the sickly perfume of the theater and the haze of booze and smoke in the lounge.

"I'm not happy," Lucy told me. "I'm sure you could tell, right?"

"I saw you were crying. I thought it was over the movie."

"If we'd stayed," she said, "you would have cried too."

"Was it that bad?"

"Yes," she said. "Yes! It was deeply bad. And on top of it

that bastard Pritchard whom I've always loved." She looked at me thoughtfully for a moment. "You know?"

"I do," I said. "We've all been there."

She looked away and laughed bitterly, as though her lofty grief must be beyond the limits of my imagination. I was annoyed, since I had hoped to divert her from pining. On the other hand, it was entertaining to watch her doing unrequited love with restraint and a touch of self-scorning irony.

"This man is deliberately trying to make me crazy," she said. "And to kill himself."

"It's a type," I explained.

"Oh yeah?" She gave me another pitying glance. "You think so?"

She had crushed my helpful routine. I put it aside. "Was that the wife?" I asked. "The blonde?"

"Yes," Lucy said. "Think she's attractive?"

"Well," I said, "on a scale of yes or no . . ."

"All right, all right," she said. "All right."

"Met her?"

"I have met her," said Lucy. "When I did, I thought, Hey, she's not a bad kid. But she's a fucking bitch, it turns out."

I kept my advice to myself, and little by little Lucy detached herself from her regrets. Later I came to know how suddenly her moods could change. It was of course an affliction, in her case untreatable. She kept her ghosts close at hand and always on call. They were present as a glimmer of surprise behind her eyes that never disappeared.

After a while I got her to walk with me; we shed our shoes and went across the moonlit beach. Brion seemed to be off her mind.

The sand at the water's edge had a steep dropoff to the

surf. We clambered down to the wet sand where the waves broke. The sea's withdrawing force was nearly enough to pull us off our feet. Lucy lost her balance and I had to put an arm around her waist to preserve her.

"It could take you away," Lucy said.

We climbed the four feet or so to the looser sand, which left us out of breath. As we walked back, Lucy told a story from her earliest days in town. She had fallen in with some fast-lane hipsters. Many of them came from industry families. One night she and a friend found themselves on the beach with the daughter of a world-famous entertainment figure. The daughter passed out, so when Lucy and her friend saw somebody coming they ran off into the nearby shadows. Two men arrived, equally world-famous. They encountered the daughter sprawled on the sand and tried to rouse her. The adolescent responded with dazed, rude mutterings. One man told the other whose daughter she was. Lucy always remembered his Viennese accent.

"*Ja*," the man said to his friend. "Kid's a valking disaster." Lucy and her friend giggled in the dark. Who could walk?

"I don't drink anymore," Lucy told me.

In spite of her solemn reflections, when we got back to the trailer she produced some Quaaludes and cocaine for me. I did a sopor and a couple of lines on her beautiful goatskin table. We drank champagne with it, which I feared would be a mistake. We were ready to get it on, both of us, but I wondered briefly if she might not suffer a morning-after-the-fact change of heart. She was a woman on the rebound; I was a stranger and afraid there might be recriminations. That was not Lucy, but I didn't know it then. She seemed so mercurial. I think we watched a little of Carson that night and found it uproariously funny in the wrong places. It was true that she smoked incessantly and smelled of tobacco. Otherwise she was a Levantine angel, one of the celestial damsels awarded to the devout and to me. In the sack she told me about her early life in Fresno.

"Know what people called Armenians?" she asked.

"What, baby?" We had gone to bed to Otis Redding, "Dock of the Bay," and there beside me Lucy addressed her après cigarette with such intensity and style that, after three years clean, I wanted one too. "Tell what they called the poor Armenians."

"They called us the Fresno Indians. Not so much people in Fresno. But in other towns. Modesto."

"How appropriate in your case."

She daintily set her smoke down, turned around and poked me in the ribs, hard, forcing me back into focus. She was wild-eyed. "Don't fucking say 'poor Armenians'! You're disrespecting my parents."

She was not really angry, although she had me fooled for a moment. She ran her fingers down my bones like a harpist and we slept the sleep of the whacked until drizzly dawn. Getting up, it struck me that I was due in New York in less than a week and what fun Lucy was. She would be on location in Mendocino until I left. This saddened our morning. We swore to keep in touch, the contemporary West Coast vow of enduring passion.

The gig in New York was the rewrite of a script that had been worked by two different writers unaware of each other's efforts. The dawning era of serious adult movies (a term that did not then altogether carry the meaning it has today) had inspired them to attempts at revolutionizing the film idiom. They both seemed to think that some ideal director would be guided by their novel scene settings and subtle dialogue. The thing had to be done in New York because the indispensable star lived in Bucks County and hated the coast. Naturally the synthesis was a turgid rat's nest and the job shameful and distressing. It was a project only God could have saved; I failed. I didn't like failing but I got paid, and thanks to Him the thing never got made. If it had, you can be sure I would have eaten the rap for it all by myself.

Then a doctoring job on a picture in production in England came my way. The project was an Englishing of a French movie for which the producers had actually paid money, and the translation of it by a British writer with a good command of French was not at all bad. But the setting had been transferred to Queens, and the producers thought his draft both too faithful to the original and too un-American. This was one to grab, though, a worthwhile credit. I went over to London, got hired and started looking for an apartment. Meanwhile the producers put me up in a crummy room at Brown's. The weather was sleety so I read my way through Olivia Manning's trilogies, Balkan and Levant. At this time Britain had little daytime television, lest weak-minded people play hooky from their dark satanic mills. For the same reason, nighttime television went off around eleven, to the national anthem.

One night I turned on the tube to see that ITV was running a soap Lucy had done two years before. The moment I recognized her I felt a rush, a fond longing. I wasn't inclined to explore the feeling. Without prejudice — I think without prejudice — I was struck by how good she was in it. She looked altogether youthful and lovely, and she had a substance in the role that was worlds away from the poor Pocahontas routine my pal John had thrust on her. Days later I watched another episode. She played a villainous character — slim sexy brunettes were usually villainesses then — who did a lot of lying. She managed to render deceit without sideward glances or eye rolling. Her character had heart and mystery. Also intelligence. Vanished were the trace elements of Valley Girl adolescence that I had become rather fond of. But I preferred Lucy the pro because in those days I loved watching real artists deliver.

Now I wonder whether it wasn't about then — that early in the game — that I started doubting myself, distrusting the quality of the silence in which I worked. Anyway, in Lucy's performance on that soap I thought I recognized the effort of one who lived for doing the voices, the way good writers did. Equipped with a sheath of fictional identity, she turned incandescent.

In the morning, I phoned her across eight time zones and tried to tell her what I had seen her do. She tried to tell me how she'd done it. Neither of us in that sudden conversation quite succeeded.

So I asked her: "How's life?"

She said: "Oh, man, don't ask me. I don't know, you know? Sometimes bearable. At others fucked."

"The pains of love or what?"

"I miss you," she said all at once, and I told her, from the heart, that I missed her too. I hadn't been asking her about us, but I can tell you she put me in the moment.

The next day I got a call from John, the perpetrator of *Unbound Unleashed Uncooked*. During my conversation with Lucy I had mentioned that I was house hunting. Now John told me that none other than Heathcliff, Brion Pritchard, had a place in St. John's Wood I could borrow for a moderate fee. I was so enthused, and tired of hearing landlords either hang up or purr with greed at the sound of an American voice, that I went for it at once. The studio that had green-lighted us paid. Distracted, I failed to focus on the distastefulness of this arrangement. Anyway, prowling and prying about the place when I should have been writing, I discovered many amusing and scandalous things about Mr. and Mrs. Heathcliff that sort of endeared them to me.

Then a strange and wonderful thing happened. One evening at the interval of a play at the Royal Court I saw a girl — she was so lovely and gamine that I could not think of that creature as anything but a girl — who was speaking American English to a female friend she had come with. I noticed that she was wearing Capezios. Catching her alone for a moment, I made my move. My predations at that time often had a theatrical background.

"You're a dancer," I told her.

She was in fact a dancer. I asked her if she cared for dinner or coffee or a drink after the play, but she didn't want to leave her friend alone. Today I would have given her my phone number, but not then, so I asked for hers and she gave it to me. On our first date we went to an Italian place in Hampstead. Jennifer had spent two years with the Frankfurt Ballet, and when we met she was in England pondering options. European cities were losing their state art subsidies, and there was no shortage of young dancers from Britain and the States. I took her home, not pressing it. Our second meeting was on Highgate Hill, and as we walked to Ken Wood we told each other the story of our lives. This was the wonder-of-me stage of our courtship and it was genuinely sweet.

It turned out that Jennifer, notwithstanding her adorable long-toothed smile and freckled nose, had been around the block, a runaway child and an exotic dancer — a teenage stripper — in New Orleans. Her nice parents in Oak Lawn had reclaimed her and sent her back to ballet school, first in Dallas, finally in New York. As a student she had gotten into cocaine and danced a *Nutcracker* in Princeton, where the falling-snow effects, she said, made her sneeze. We were so easy with each other, at the same time so intoxicated. It was lovely.

In London, although there was plenty of blow about, she abstained, and in that hard-drinking city she stayed sober. She put up with my boozing, but sweetly let me know she did not want to see the other. I thought often about moving her into the place in St. John's Wood. Since the Pritchards showed no sign of returning, I had stayed in it after the script was done and kept it on my own for months afterward, working on originals. For some reason we never got to the point of moving in together that year. Then I got a call — like all your Hollywood Calling calls, it came in the middle of the night — asking me if I would come out and talk about another deathless number. I decided to go, and when I told Jennifer, she cried.

"I thought we were long-term."

It just about broke my heart. "We are long-term," I hastened to say. I wondered if she would ask to come with me. I probably would have taken her. At the same time, I wanted to see Lucy.

Back in L.A., it was a dry, sunny winter inland with a mellow marine layer at the beach each morning. The place I liked that I could have was a condo in Laguna. Laguna was prettier then, but for some reason I had not known about the traffic and had not realized what was happening to Orange County. The apartment overlooked the sea and had sunsets.

I had batted out three original scripts in London. Mysteriously, the first two drew from my then agent — Mike? Marty? — more apparent sympathy than admiration. Out in the movie world, two of the three were promptly skunked. I was still used to being the boy wonder, and a midlife bout of rejection was unappealing. I didn't much like rejection. Maybe I had tried too hard, attempting to scale the new peaks of serious and adult, naively imagining for myself an autonomy that neither I nor anyone in the industry possessed. The third one, anyway, was optioned, went into turnaround and years later actually got made. But my deathless number expired.

Frustrated and depressed, I postponed calling Lucy. During my third week back I finally invited her down for another walk on the beach.

Climbing out of her dusty Jag, she looked nothing but fine. She wore turquoise and a deerskin jacket, my Fresno Indian. With her smooth tan, her skin was the color of coffee ice cream and her eyes were bright. Ever since watching her perform in the soap I had begun to think of her as beautiful.

As we set out down the beach, beside the Pacific again, she put on a baseball cap that said "Hussong's Cantina," promoting the joint in Ensenada. It was a sunny day even at the shore, and you might have called the sea sparkling. A pod of dolphins patrolled outside the point break, gliding on air, making everything in life look easy. Lucy told me she had tested for a part in our friend John's next movie, a horror picture. She was still worried about whether he had spotted the two of us walking out of Grauman's. The horror flick sounded like another bomb at best. This time Lucy had read the shooting script and knew what there was to know of the plot.

"She's a best friend. Supposed to be cute and funny. She dies."

I said that in my opinion she, Lucy, was ready for comedy.

"Tom, everyone pretty much dies horribly except the leads. It's a horror flick."

We had a nice day and night.

A week later I went up to Silver Lake, where Lucy had moved after selling her trailer in Malibu. Her bungalow had some plants out front with an orangy spotlight playing on them, and in its beam I saw that the glass panels on her front door were smashed and the shards scattered across her doorway. Among them were pieces of what looked like a dun-colored Mexican pot. This was all alarming, since her door would now admit all that lived, crawled and trawled in greater L.A. Moreover, there was blood. When she let me in

I asked her about it but got no answer. She brought us drinks and I lit a joint I had brought and she began to cry. Suddenly she gave me a sly smile that in the half darkness of the patio reminded me of the weeping Indian maid I had rescued on the next seat at Grauman's.

"I'm in difficulty," she said.

I said I could see that. It turned out to be all about bloody Heathcliff, Brion Pritchard, still on the scene and newly cast in the horror movie. Third-rate art was staggering toward real life again: Brion was the man who got to stab her repeatedly in the forthcoming vehicle.

"How can they do that?" I asked her. "Another of John's movies and Pritchard gets to kill you again. Isn't that like stupid?"

"He's relentless," she said. "Tommy, don't ask! What do I know?"

I suppose it was I who should have known. Brion was in serious decline, succumbing to occupational ailments in a tradition that went back to the time of nickelodeons. He drank. A man of robust appetites, he also smoked and snorted and stuffed and swallowed. On top of it all, he had started lifting weights and pioneering steroids. He boozed all day and through the night, drove drunk, punched some of the wrong people. Along the Rialto, all this was being noted and remarked upon. He was a violent working-class guy, one of A. E. Houseman's beautiful doomed ploughboys, who but for talent and fortune would have drunk himself into Penrhyndeudraeth churchyard long before. Predictably, he had identified Lucy as the font of his troubles.

Shortly after dawn on the morning before my visit, Brion had come banging on Lucy's door, haranguing her in elegant

English and low Welsh. Impatient to enter and mess with her, he had taken her ornamental pot and shoved in the door, cutting himself in the process, badly enough to sober him slightly and slow him down. This bought time for Lucy to call 911. She told me that when the cops came Brion gave them the old Royal Shakespeare, which by then in Hollywoodland impressed no one. They all but begged her to press charges, although he had succeeded in hitting her only once, hard. Naturally she denied it heroically — I could well picture her playing that one — and sent them away. At least she hadn't raced to his side at the hospital.

That evening it was plain we were not going to have much of a party. I asked Lucy to come down to Laguna with me. She dawdled and I hung around until she turned me out. I was angry; moreover, I was feeling too much like what you might call a confidant. In the end I made her swear to get the door fixed or replaced, and I said I'd do it if she wouldn't. I told her to call the cops and me if the loutish Welshman accosted her again. I have to admit that if it came to action, I wanted the cops on my side.

Driving back that night I was unhappy. I had expected to stay with her. I should mention that in this period there occurred the last brief gas panic — odd- and even-numbered days and so on. In my opinion the fuel shortages of those years played their part in the vagaries of romance. People often went to bed with each other because their gas tanks were low.

I picked up work at that point with HBO, which had then started showing its own productions. The project involved several interviews around the country in the subjects' hometowns. It was a Vietnam War story, echoing the anger of the recent past. This took me out of town for the next three weeks. In a hotel in Minneapolis I picked up a *USA Today* with a back-page story announcing that Brion Pritchard was dead. It was shocking, of course, but in fact with the advent of AIDS a sense of mortality increasingly pervaded. We could not know it, but death was coming big-time. In that innocent age no one had imagined that anything more serious would happen to Brion than his dropping a barbell on his foot. I felt nothing at first, no relief, no regret. He was no friend of mine. On the way back to L.A., though, I became drunk and depressed, as if a fellow circus performer had fallen from a high wire. All of us worked without a net.

I had some doubts about calling Lucy too soon, mainly because I no longer fancied the role of consoler. Eventually I realized that if I wanted to see her again, I would have to endure it. When I called she sounded more confused than stricken. At first I couldn't be sure I had the right person on the line. My thought was: She doesn't know how she feels. This is a role thrust on her, and her feelings are down in some dark inaccessible region much overlaid. With what? Childish hungers, history, drama school? Capped by unacknowledged work and guilty ambition. A little undeserved notoriety of the tabloid sort. By then I thought I knew a few things about actors. I had been one myself years before.

When I saw Lucy next she gave a display of what I now recognized as false cheer. In this dangerous state she could appear downright joyous. When I expressed sympathy over Brion she gave me an utterly blank look. Being the pro she was, Lucy was almost always aware of how she looked, but the expression she showed me was unpremeditated, unintentionally conveying to me that Pritchard's death was literally none of my business, that neither I nor anyone else shared enough common ground with her and the late Heathcliff, *ensemble*, for even polite condolences. But somehow, a couple of weeks later we found ourselves on the road to Ensenada. Ensenada and Tijuana could still be raggedy fun in those days. We managed to borrow a warped convertible from an actor pal and took off down the coast road. I hope we told him we were crossing the border.

The drive was an idyll, precisely defined, I was unsurprised to learn, as a happy episode, typically an idealized or unsustainable one. Down south that April afternoon there were still a few blossoming orange groves to mix memory and desire on the ocean breeze. Over the emerald cliffs people were hang-gliding, boys and alpha girls swooping like buzzards on the updrafts. In the sea below surfers were bobbing, pawing ahead of the rollers to catch the curl. And on the right, a gorgeous gilded — no, golden — dome displayed a sign that read, as I recall, SELF-REALIZATION GOLDEN WORLD FELLOWSHIP. It was the place the surfer kids called Yogi Beach, and there we overcame Lucy's peculiar grief and spent the happiest half day of our lives.

In Tijuana, which was as far as we got, we put the convertible in Caesar's protected parking and ate the good steak and the famous salad. We did not talk about Brion. For a while we traded recollections of Brooklyn College drama school, where, strangely, both of us had put in time.

It seemed, as the day lengthened, that the elations of our trip stirred a mutual yearning. Not about the night, because of course the night would be ours. I thought we might find our way through the dazzle of our confusions to something beyond. In my memory of that day — or in my fond dream of a memory — I was about to guide us there. In this waking dream I'm suspended at the edge of a gesture or the right words. All at once a glimmer of caution flickers, goes out, flashes again. Who was she, after all? An actor, above all. I was wary of how she brought out the performer in me. I mean the performer at the core, ready to follow her out on the wire where she lived her life. At that age I thought I might walk it too.

I could have been a moment short of giving her the sign she wanted, whatever it was. These days I sometimes imagine that with the right words, a touch, a look, I might have snatched her out of disaster's path, away from the oncoming life that was gathering ahead of her. I held back. Surely that was wise. The moment passed and then Lucy simply got distracted.

I let us drift down the colonnades of the *farmacia* tour at the busy end of Revolución, chasing green crosses and phosphorescence. I wanted a party too. Joy's hand, they say, is always at his lips bidding adieu. That melancholy truth drove us.

We crossed back to Yanquilandia without incident. On the drive up the freeway we talked about ourselves.

"You and me," Lucy asked. "What is *that?*"

I didn't know. I said it was a good thing.

"Where would it go?"

Not into the sunset, I thought. I said exactly that. Lucy was ripped. She chattered.

"Everything goes there," she told me.

I ought not to have been driving. I was stoned myself.

As Lucy talked on I kept changing the subject, or at least tweaking it.

"I have a kind of plan for my life," she said. "Part of it is career shit." She had picked up the contemporary habit of referring to people's film and stage work that way, including her own. As in "I want to get my shit up there." Or "I saw you in whatever it was and I loved your shit." It was thought to be unpretentious and hip, one social deviant to another. I particularly hated it, perhaps for pertinent but at the time unconscious reasons. "Actually," she went on with an embarrassed laugh, "artistic ambitions."

"Why not?"

Her fancies involved going east, to off-Broadway. Or working in Europe. Or doing something in one of the independent productions that were beginning to find distribution. Besides the artistic ambitions she entertained some secular schemes for earning lots of money in pictures. In retrospect, these were unrealistic. We found ourselves back on the subject of us.

"Don't you love me?" she asked.

"You know I do."

"I hope so. You're the only one who ever knew I was real."

I politely denied that, but I thought about it frequently thereafter.

"What about Brion?"

"Poor Brion was a phantom himself," she said.

"Really? He threw a pretty solid punch for a phantom."

"I wasn't there that time either," she said. "I hardly felt it."

As we passed the refinery lights of Long Beach, she shook her head as though she were trying to clear it of whispers.

"You know," she said, "as far as shadows and ghosts go, I fear my own."

"I understand," I said. Hearing her say it chilled me, but for some reason I *did* understand, thoroughly. I was coming to know her as well as was possible.

"Why do you always treat me with tea-party manners, Tom?"

"I don't. I don't even know what you mean."

"You're always trying to be funny."

I said that didn't mean I didn't love her. "It's all I know," I said.

We were driving along the margins of a tank farm that stood beside the freeway. Its barbed chain-link fence was lined with harsh prison-yard arc lights that lit our car interior as we passed and framed us in successive bursts of white glare. In my delusion, the light put me in mind of overbright motel corridors with stained walls tunneling through gnomish darkness. My head hurt. In the spattered white flashes I caught her watching me. I thought I could see the reflected arc lights in her eyes and the enlarged pupils almost covering their irises, black on black.

"Everybody loves you, Tom," she said. "Don't they?"

How sad and lonely that made me feel. Out of selfishness and need I grieved for myself. It passed.

"Yes, I'm sure everyone does. It's great."

"Do I count?" she asked.

Yes and no. But of course I didn't say that. In the twisted light I saw her out there sauntering toward a brass horizon and I wanted to follow after. But I was not so foolish nor had I the generosity of spirit. I was running out of heart.

"You more than anyone, Lucy," I said. "Only you, really."

That's how I remember it. As we drove on Lucy began to complain about a letter she said I'd written.

"You used these exquisite phrases. Avoiding the nitty-gritty. All fancy dancing."

"I don't do that. I don't know what letter you mean. Come on — 'exquisite phrases'?" I laughed at her.

A couple of miles later she informed me she had written the letter to herself. "In your style," she said.

"So," I asked her, "what were the phrases you liked?"

"I don't remember. I wanted to get it down. The way you are."

"Lucy, please don't write letters from me to yourself. I can do it."

"You never wrote me," she said, which I guess was partly the point. "Anyone can jump out of a phone."

Suddenly, but without apparent spite, she declared, "John's going to expand my part." She was talking about the now revived horror movie in which John had hired a live British actor to strangle her. However, on consideration she thought he might transform her into a surviving heroine. I said it was great but that it probably wouldn't be as much fun.

"You know," she said, "you don't get credit for being scared and dying. It doesn't count as acting. Anyway, I can live without fun."

"If you say so."

"John," she said, "wants to marry me." For some reason, at that point she put her hand on my knee and turned her face to me. "Seriously."

I wondered about that in the weeks following. Once she showed me a postcard of the Empire State Building he had sent her from New York. He had adorned it with embarrassing jokey scribbles about his erection. One day I took John to Musso's for lunch but he said not a word to me about her. Over our pasta I asked him if it was true that he was sparing Lucy's character in the thing forthcoming.

"Oh," he said, as though it were something that had slipped his mind. "Absolutely. Lucy's time has come."

I suspected that the lead would be the kind of supposed-to-be-feisty female lately appearing as part of the serious and adult wave. I knew Lucy would deliver that one all the way from Avenida Revolución.

"She can give a character some inner aspects," I told him.

"You're so right."

"Good actress," I suggested. "Great kid."

John went radiant, but he didn't look like a bridegroom to me. "You know it, Tom. Tops."

He didn't marry Lucy. Instead, when the funeral-baked meats had cooled he married Brion Pritchard's widow, Maerwyn. He didn't even promote Lucy to insipid ingénue. Halfway through the horror movie her character died like a trouper. In spite of my infatuation, I had to admit there were many great things one could do with Lucy, but marrying her was probably not one of them.

We went out a few times. She began to seem to me — for lack of a better word — unreal. I kept trying to get close to her again. At the time I was selling neither scripts nor story ideas. There were no calls. I might have tried for an acting gig; I was owed a few favors. I had no illusions about my talent, but I was cheap and willing, well spoken enough for walk-ons as a mad monk or warmongering general. I offered a Brooklyn Heights accent, which sounds not at all the way you think. But I had grown self-conscious and all the yoga in the world wasn't going to bring back my chops or my youthful arrogance. That was what I'd need in front of a camera. My main drawback as an actor had always been a tendency to perform from the neck up. I might have thrived in the great days of radio.

Eventually I got a job with a newspaper chain working as their "West Coast editor." It took up a lot of my time, and part of my work was resisting being transformed into a gossip columnist. I almost got fired for doing a piece for the *New York Times* Arts and Leisure section. The news chain paid a lot less than writing for the movies, but it paid regularly. I had plans to engineer a spread for Lucy, but nothing came along to hang it on.

Out of what seemed like nowhere, she took up with a friend of mine named Asa Maclure, pronounced *Mac*-lure, whom people called Ace. Ace was an actor and occasional writer (mostly of blaxploitation flix during the seventies) with whom I had liked to go out drinking and drugging and what we insensitively called wenching. Ace was a wild man. What inclined me to forgive him all was a telegram he had once sent to a director in Washington for whom he was going to act Othello: CANT WAIT TO GET MY HANDS AROUND THAT WHITE WOMANS THROAT.

Ace had just arrived back in L.A. from Africa, where he

had portrayed a loyal askari who saved a blond white child from swart Moorish bandits in the Sahara. The child, supposed to be French, was from eastern Europe somewhere. Ace was unclear as to which country. She had gone on location with her mother along as chaperone. The mom was, as Ace put it, a babe. Ace was suave and beautiful, the kind of guy they would cast as Othello. In no time at all his romance, as they say, with Mrs. Vraniuk was the talk of every location poker game. Restless under the desert sky, Ace decided to shift his attention to young Miss Vraniuk. Consummation followed, producing some uneasiness since the kid was not yet twenty-one. Nor was she eighteen. Nor, it seemed, perhaps, was she fifteen. But it was in another country, another century, a different world. At the time, in the circumstances, it represented no more than a merry tale.

"This child was ageless, man," Ace told us. "She had the wiles of Eve."

If any images or other evidence of desert passion existed, no one worried much about it. Talk was cheap. And most American tabloids then did not even buy pictures.

Ace and Lucy became a prominent item, appearing in the very papers that now employed me. The stories were fueled by Ace's sudden trajectory toward stardom. Though she was blooming, grew more beautiful as she aged, Lucy was noticed only as Ace's companion.

It happened that one week the papers dispatched me with a photographer to do a story on kids in South Central who rode high-stakes bike races. The races ran on barrio streets, inviting the wagers of high-rolling meth barons and senior gangbangers. Lucy decided to come with me, and when I went down a second time she came along again. Both times she seemed a little hammered and could not be discouraged from flirting with a few speed-addled pistoleros. A local actually approached me with a warning that she was behaving unwisely. Driving back to Silver Lake, she said: "You and I are sleepwalking."

"How do you mean?" I asked her.

"We're unconscious. Living parallel lives. We never see each other."

I said I thought she was involved with Ace.

"I mean really see each other, Tommy. The way people can see each other."

"You're the one who's sleepwalking, Lucy."

"Oh," she said, "don't say that about me." She sounded as if she had been caught out, trapped in something like a lie. "That's frightening."

"That's what you said about both of us. I thought you were on to something."

Maybe she was confounded by her own inconsistency. More likely she never got there. She sat silent for a while. Then she said: "Don't you understand, Tommy? It's always you with me. Ever since Grauman's."

It was not a joke. I don't think she meant to hurt or deceive me with the things she said. For some reason, though, she could leave me feeling abandoned and without hope. Not only about us but about everything. She was concerned with being there. And with whom to be. It occurred to me that perhaps she was going through life without, in a sense, knowing what she was doing. Or that she was not doing anything but forever being done. Waiting for a cue, a line, a vehicle, marks, blocking. Somewhere to stand and be whoever she might decide she was, even for a moment.

"That can't be true, Lucy."

"Oh, yes," she said, urgently, deeply disturbed. "Oh, yes, baby, it is true."

There was no point in arguing. A couple of miles along, she put her hand on my driving arm, holding it hard, and I suspected she might force the wheel.

"I have such strength," she said. "I don't know how to use it. Or when. I accommodate. That's the trouble."

One strange afternoon, Asa Maclure, Lucy and I decided to go bungee jumping. Seriously. It might have represented the zenith of our tattered glory days. The place we chose to jump from was a mountainside high above the desert, reachable by tram from Palm Springs. There, over a rock face that rose a sheer few hundred feet from the valley floor, two actual Australians, a boy and a girl, had the jump concession.

I might say that I can't imagine how we came to plan this, but in fact I know how. Ace was well aware of the fraught status between Lucy and me. I'm sure she talked about me to him, maybe a lot. He would tease me, or both of us, when we were together.

"You all are pathetic," he declared once. "A gruesome twosome. Tommy, she sighs and pines over you. I believe you do the same. I don't mind."

I was provoked. He was saying that our strange affair notwithstanding, he — Mister Mens Sana in Corpore Sano — was the one she turned to for good loving. It was a taunt. So I decided I'd play some soul poker with him for Lucy and win and take her away. Thereafter he tried to see that she avoided me. When we were all together Ace and I would watch each other for cracks in which to place a wedge. Though I liked to believe I was smarter than Ace, he was verbally quite agile.

The bungee incident began as a bad joke and started overheating, the way one kid's playful punch of another will gradually lead to an angry fistfight. In fact it was completely childish, nothing less than a dare. It was I who made the mistake of talking bungee-jump; I'd seen the Australians referred to in the *Times*'s weekend supplement and it occurred to me I might get my employers to pay for us. Ace was famous, Lucy semifamous, beginning to get noticed, frequently called in to test, and cast at times to help lesser actors look good. There were also reruns of her several soaps.

I felt I had to do this. I had made a jocular reference to this scheme in the presence of Ace, and Lucy and Ace called me on it. While I was trying to prod the powers above to spring and assign a photographer, the two of them went and did it. Would Lucy descend into the ponderosa-scented void after her paramour? A thing never in question. It was an eminence she'd sought lifelong, a Fuji-disposable Lover's Leap. They survived.

All my life I have regretted not being there. For one thing, regarding *Mac*lure, I held my manhood cheap. He had foxed me and bonded with her in a way that I, who had made something of a career out of witnessing Lucy's beau gestes, would never experience. She hurt me bad.

Suffering is illuminating, as they say, and in my pain I almost learned something about myself. I repressed the insight. I was not ready, then, to yield to it.

"I wanted it to be you," Lucy said, like a deflowered prom

queen apologizing to the high school athlete whose lettered jersey she had worn and dishonored.

"I wanted it to be me too," I said. "Why did you go and do it?"

"I was afraid I wouldn't do it if we waited."

I shouted at her, something I very rarely did.

"You'd have done it with me! You goddamn well would have!"

Of course this exchange was as juvenile as the rest of the incident, but it stirred the unconsidered home truth I had been resisting. This kind of juvenility goes deep, and you can also approach self-awareness after acting childishly.

Still, I wasn't up to facing it. For days and days I went to sleep stoned, half drunk, whispering: What was it like, Lucy? I meant the leap. I very nearly went bungee jumping by myself, but it seemed a sterile exercise.

I was bitter. I had excuses to avoid her and I used them all. She called me at the office and in Laguna, but I was tired of it. The next thing I knew I had quit my job and gone over to England to find Jennifer.

Jen had got a Green Book and was teaching dance with some friends in Chester. When we saw each other I knew it was on again. I had to peel her loose from some painter from over the border. Another fucking Welsh boyfriend!

I took her home to Dallas and met the high-toned folks and married her in the high-toned Episcopal equivalent of a nuptial Mass, dressed up like a character out of Oscar Wilde. She conscientiously wore red, though I pointed out that neither of us had been married before. We moved to Laguna and, lovely and smart as she was, Jen got herself a tenure-track job in dance at UC San Diego. I watched her work, and she was peppy and the good-cop bad-cop kind of teacher, and you never saw a prettier backside in a leotard. We moved to Encinitas.

My bride all but supported me while I worked on a few scripts. She had loans from her parents and the UC salary. I don't know exactly what had changed in the movie business; I hadn't noticed anything good. However, I optioned two scripts right away.

One day I was coming out of the HBO offices on Olympic when I ran into Asa Maclure. The sight of him froze my heart. In those years you knew what the way he looked meant. He was altogether too thin for his big frame; his cool drape sagged around him. The worst of it was his voice, always rich, Shakespearean, his preacher father's voice. It had become a rasp. He sounded old and he looked sad and wise, a demeanor that he used to assume in jest. I hoped he wouldn't mention the bungee jump, but he did. Plainly it meant a lot to him. From a different perspective, it did to me too. We traded a few marginally insincere laughs about how absurd the whole thing had been. He looked so doomed I couldn't begrudge him the high they must have had. I didn't ask him how he was.

A couple of weeks later I got a call from Lucy, and she wanted to see me. She was still in Silver Lake. I lied to Jennifer when I drove up to visit Lucy. Jen had not asked where I was going, but I volunteered false information. I felt profoundly unfaithful, though I realized that there was not much likelihood of my sleeping with Lucy. No possibility at all, from my point of view. So I felt unfaithful to her too.

Lucy, in Silver Lake, seemed at once agitated and exhausted.

"Ace said he saw you," she told me when we were seated on the patio dead Heathcliff had demolished.

Passing through her living room I noticed that the house was in a squalid state. The floors were littered with plastic flowers and charred metal cylinders. There were roaches on the floor and in the ashtrays, along with beer cans and other post-party knickknacks. Lucy had been running with a new set of friends. I imagined these people as a kind of simian troop, although I never got it clear who exactly they were and how Lucy had been impressed into being their hostess. I did know that it had somehow to do with supply and demand.

I had been out of town and was not familiar with freebasing. I can't be sure that Asa turned her on to it. Basing was the rage then in extremist circles like his. She talked about it with a rapturous smile. I had been around long enough to remember when street drugs hit the industry big-time, and I remembered that smile from the days when each new advance in narcosis had been acclaimed as somebody's personal Fourth of July. A life-changing event. To cool the rock's edges Lucy had taken to easing down behind a few upscale pharmaceuticals: 'ludes, opiate pills. Unfortunately for all of us, genuine Quaaludes were disappearing, even south of the border. This left the opiates, which were still dispensed with relative liberality. While I watched, Lucy cooked up the brew in her kitchen as she had been instructed. She told me she had always liked to cook, though this was a side of her I'd never seen.

Cooking base, we ancients of art will recall, involved a number of tools. 7-Elevens then sold single artificial flowers in test-tube-like containers, so that crack scenes were sometimes adorned with sad, false blossoms. Lucy mixed quite a few gram baggies with baking soda and heated them in a cunning little Oriental pot. The devil of details was in the mix, which Lucy approached with brisk confidence. Alarmingly, the coke turned into viscous liquid. People who have put in time in really crappy motels may recall finding burned pieces of coat hanger on the floor of the closets or wardrobes. Lucy had one, and she used it to fish the brew out so it could cool and congeal. It was then that the stem came into play, and a plastic baby bottle, and a burned wad of Chore Boy. On the business end of the stem, appropriately enough, was the bottle's nipple, which the adept lipped like a grouper on brain coral.

We did it and at first it reminded me of how, when I was a child, my mother would have me inhale pine needle oil to cure a chest cold. The effect of freebasing was different, although if someone had told me it cured colds I wouldn't have argued. It was quite blissful for a time and we were impelled toward animated chatter. I commenced to instruct Lucy on the joys of marriage, for which I was then an enthusiast. She soared with me; her eyes flashed. In this state she was always something to see.

"I'm so happy for you. No, I'm really not. Yes I am."

We smoked for an hour or more. As she plied the hanger end to scrape residue from the filter and stem, she told me about her career prospects, which seemed stellar. She had been cast for what seemed a good part in a film by a notori-

ously eccentric but gifted director who had assembled a kind
of repertory company for his pictures. Some of these made
money, some tanked, but all of them got some respect. For
Lucy, this job was a good thing. And not only was there the
film part. As schedules permitted, she was going to do Elena
in *Uncle Vanya* at a prestigious neighborhood playhouse. I
rejoiced for her. As I was leaving, supremely confident and
looking forward to the drive, I kissed her. Her response
seemed less sensual than emotional. I was hurt, although I
had no intention of suggesting anything beyond our embrace. Sometimes you just don't know what you want.

Around Westminster, I began to feel the dive. Its sensation was accompanied by a sudden suspicion that Lucy's re-
versal of fortune might be a little too good to be true. When
I got home I took two pain pills and believed her again.

Not long after this we read that Asa Maclure was dead.
He had AIDS all right, but it wasn't the disease that killed
him. The proximate cause of his death was an accident oc-
casioned by his unsteady attempt to cook some base. He set
himself on fire, ran as fast as he could manage out of his San
Vicente apartment and took off down the unpeopled sidewalks of the boulevard. He ran toward the ocean. Hundreds
of cars passed him as he ran burning. According to one al-
leged witness, even a fire truck went by, but that may have
been someone's stroke of cruel wit.

Asa Maclure was a wonderful man. He was, as they say, a
damn good actor. He was also enormous fun. In the end,
he was a good friend too, although obviously a difficult one.
Suffice it to say I mourned him.

Jennifer and I went to his funeral. It was held at a freshly painted but rickety-looking black church in what had once been a small southern town not thirty miles from where her parents lived in Oak Lawn. Asa's father presided, his master in declamation. Asa had resembled his father, and the man was strong and prevailed over his grief. There were a few people from the industry, mostly African American, all male. Praise God, Lucy did not appear.

Back in Dallas at my in-laws' stately home, we had a few bourbons.

"Your friend has the kiss of death," Jennifer said. She delivered this observation without inflection, but it remained to hover on the magnolia-scented air of that cool, exquisitely tasteful room.

Both of my optioned scripts were being green-lighted.

From what I read in the papers it seemed Lucy had been replaced in the mad genius's picture. The neighborhood production of *Vanya* opened with no mention of her. I presumed she had read for it. Maybe she had assumed the part was hers. Once I met her for a sandwich in a Beverly Hills deli and we talked about Ace's death. Lucy spoke slowly, with great precision, and was obviously high. I was worried about her and also concerned to discover where Ace's death had left her.

"I've compartmentalized my life," she declared. She had brought with her a huge paperback book with dog-eared pages and she showed it to me. It was a collection of drawings by Giovanni Piranesi that featured his series called *Imaginary Prisons*, in which tiers of prison cells are ranked along Gothic stone staircases and upon the battlements of vast dungeons that ascend and descend over spaces that appear infinite. For reasons that many art lovers will immediately comprehend on seeing some of his drawings, Piranesi is a great favorite among cultivated junkies. His prisons are like their world.

On the blank pages in the book Lucy had written what she called plans. These were listed in columns, each laid out in variously colored inks and displaying Lucy's runic but attractive handwriting. When she handed the book to me for comment I could only utter a few appreciative sounds. Every word in every paragraph of every column was unreadable. I still have no idea what she had written there. Finally I could not, for my life, keep myself from saying something meant to be friendly and comforting about Asa. I got the same cold suffering look I had seen when Brion Pritchard died.

In the weeks after that, in a craven fashion, I kept my distance from her because I was afraid of what I might see and hear. She didn't call. Also the trip to Texas had left Jen and me closer somehow — at least for a while.

A few months later Lucy left a message on our machine, absurdly pretending to be someone else. Suddenly I thought I wanted to see her again. The desire, the impulse, came over me all at once in the middle of a working afternoon. On reexamination, I think the urge was partly romantic, partly Pavlovian. I was concerned. I wanted to help her. I wanted to get seriously high with her because Jen didn't use. So my trip back to Silver Lake was speeded by a blend of high-mindedness and base self-indulgence. It's a fallen world, is it not? We carry love in earthen vessels.

Lucy's house was not as dirty and disorderly as it had been on my previous visit, but everything still looked rather dingy. She did not garden or wash windows; she no longer employed her help. And she no longer cooked, since crack, the industrialized version of base, had obviated that necessity. It was safer too and far less messy than basing. The rocks went straight from the baggie into the stem. For me the hit was even better. She had Percocet and Xanax for coming down, a lot of them. She was still very attractive, and I later learned she had a thing going with a druggy doc in Beverly Hills who must have been something of an adventurer.

"I'm going to Jerusalem!" she said. She said it so joyously that for a second I thought she had got herself saved by some goof.

"Yes?" I approved wholeheartedly. Seconds after the pipe, I approved of nearly everything that way. "How great!"

"Listen to this!" she said. "I'm going there to live in the Armenian quarter. In a monastery. Or, like, a convent."

"Terrific! As a nun?"

She laughed, and I did too. We laughed loud and long. When we were finished laughing she slapped me on the shoulder.

"No, ridiculous one! As research. Because I'm going to do a script about the massacres. I'm going to sneak into Anatolia and see the Euphrates."

She had an uncle who was a high-ranking priest at the see of the Jerusalem patriarch. He would arrange for her stay, and she could interview survivors of the slaughter.

"I want to do this for my parents. For my background. I won't say 'heritage' because that's so pretentious."

"I think it's a great idea."

I was about, in my boisterous good humor, to call her project a pipe dream. Fortunately I thought better of it.

She saw the thing as eminently possible. The Russians had unraveled and she might film in Armenia. There were prominent Armenian Americans in the movie business, in town and in the former USSR. She had me about a quarter convinced, though I wondered about the writing. She had the answer to that.

"This is yours, Tommy! Will you do it? Will you go with me? Will you think about it? Please? Because if you wrote it I'm sure I could direct. Because you know how it is. You and me."

Naturally the urgency was intense. "It's a sweet idea," I said.

"You could bring your wife, you know. I forget her name."

I told her. She had somehow deduced that Jennifer was younger than she.

"They're all named Jennifer," she said.

As if to bind me to the plan, she pressed huge handfuls of Percocet on me. Starting to drive home, I realized that I was too rattled to make it all the way to Encinitas. I checked into a motel that was an island of downscale on the Westwood–Santa Monica border and called Jen, home from her classes. I explained how I had come up to inquire into something or other and suddenly felt too ill to make it back that evening.

"Don't drive then," Jen said. I could see trouble shimmering on the blacktop ahead.

Next Lucy disappeared. Her phone was suddenly out of service. The next time I was up in town I went to her house and found it unoccupied. The front garden was ochre rubble and the house itself enclosed in scaffolding. It was lunchtime, and a work crew of Mesoamericans in faded flannel shirts were eating In-N-Out burgers on the roof.

Once I got a message in which she claimed to be in New York. It was rambling and unsound. She said some indiscreetly affectionate things but neglected to leave a number or address. I did my best to tape over the message, to stay out of trouble. I had only partial success.

A little serendipity followed. I heard from a friend in New York, a documentary filmmaker, whom I hadn't seen in many years. He had gone into a boutique on Madison and met the gorgeous salesperson. She seemed glamorous and mysterious and dressed enticingly from the store, so he asked her out. He thought she might go for a Stoppard play, so he took her to the play and to the Russian Tea Room and then to Nell's. People recognized her. It turned out she was an actor, a smart actor, and could talk Stoppard with insight. She was a wild but inspired dancer and had nearly nailed a part in a Broadway play. She knew me, was in fact a friend of mine.

"Oh," I said. "Lucy."

He was disappointed she hadn't asked him home that night. Casual couplings were not completely out of fashion by then, though white balloons were beginning to ascend over West Eleventh Street. My friend thought he liked her very much, but when he'd called one evening she sounded strange. It sounded, too, as if she lived in a hotel.

I thought I knew the story, and I was right. She could hardly have asked him home because home then was an SRO on 123rd and Broadway and he would not have en-

joyed the milieu. All her salary and commissions, as I later
learned, were going for crack and for scag to mellow it out.
Pain pills were not doing it any longer. I quoted him the
maxim made famous by Nelson Algren: "Never go to bed
with someone who has more problems than you do." He
understood. I didn't think I had deprived anyone of their
bliss.

There was something more to my friendly cautioning. It
wasn't exactly jealousy. It was that somehow I thought I was
the only one who could handle Lucy. That she was my par-
ish.

When she showed up in California again it was in San
Francisco. I got a call from her up there, and this time I
didn't bother to erase it. Jennifer and I were in trouble. I
had a bit of a drug problem. I was drinking a lot. I suspected
her of having an affair with some washed-up Bosnian ballet
dancer she had hired down at UCSD. The fellow was supposed to be gay, but I was suspicious. Jennifer was a well-
bred, well-spoken East Texas hardass a couple of generations
past sharecropping. Amazingly, the more I drank and used,
the more she lost respect for me. At the same time I was selling scripts like crazy, rewriting them, sometimes going out
on location to work them through. Jennifer was largely un-
impressed. Everything was stressful.

I was full of anger and junkie righteousness and I went up
to see Lucy, hardly bothering to cover my tracks. She had
rented an apartment there that belonged to her stockbroker
sister, not a bad place at all despite its being in the dreary
Haight. I guess I had wanted a look at who Lucy's latest
friends were.

Her live-in friend was Scott, and she introduced us. I had

expected a repellent creep. Scott surpassed my grisliest expectations. He had watery eyes, of a blue so pale that his irises seemed at the point of turning white. He had very thin, trembly red lips that crawled up his teeth at one corner to form a tentative sneer. He had what my mother would have called a weak chin, which she believed was characteristic of non-Anglo-Saxons. There were no other features I recall.

Scott was under the impression that he could play the guitar. He plinked on one for us as we watched and waited. Lucy avoided eye contact with me. As Scott played, his face assumed a fanatical spirituality and he rolled his strange eyes. Watching him do it induced in the beholder something like motion sickness. In his transport he suggested the kind of Jehovah's Witness who would kill you with a hammer for rejecting his *Watchtower*.

When he had finished, Lucy exclaimed, "Oh, wow." By force of will I prevented us from applauding.

Scott's poison was methamphetamine. I was not yet familiar with the drug's attraction, and this youth served as an exemplar. Having shot some, his expression shifted from visionary to scornful to paranoid and back. I had seen many druggy people over the years — I knew I was one myself — but Scott was a caution to cats. To compare his state with a mad Witness missionary was demeaning to believers. His transcendent expression, his transport, ecstasy, whatever, was centered on neurological sensation like a laboratory rat's. The mandala at the core of his universe was his own asshole. It was outrageous. However, there we were, beautiful Lucy, cultivated me, livers of the examined life, in more or less the same maze. What did it make us?

When Scott had exhausted conversation by confusing himself beyond explication, he picked up a pair of sunglasses from the floor beside him, put them on and moved them up on his forehead.

"I invented this," he told us, "this pushing-shades-up-on-your-head thing."

Weeks later, Scott was removed from her apartment with the aid of police officers, screaming about insects and imitating one. It was history repeating itself as farce, a particularly unfunny one. Lucy lost the place and the stockbroker sister was forced out. The upside was losing Scott as well.

Back home it was cold, and Jennifer grew suspicious and discontent. When she was angry her mild, educated Anglo-southern tones could tighten and faintly echo the speech of her ancestors in the Dust Bowl. Sometimes her vowels would twist themselves into the sorrowful whine of pious stump farmers abandoned by Jesus in the bottomland. You had to listen closely to detect it. I had never heard the word "honey" sound so leaden until Jennifer smacked me in the mouth with it. She could do the same thing with "dear." Dust bowl, I thought, was by then a useful metaphor for our married state.

I started going to bars. I listened to production assistants' stories about the new-style dating services. I did not pursue these routes because I was no longer so young and beautiful and because I was bitter and depressed. I did have a few one- or two-nighters on location. The best, carnally speaking, was with a stuntwoman with a body like a Mexican comic-book heroine who, it was said, had once beaten an Arizona policeman half to death. Of course bodies like hers were not rare in movieland. Straight stuntwomen were more fun, at least for me, than actresses. What they might lack in psychological dimension they made up for in contoured heft and feel and originality. They were sometimes otherwise limited, unless you counted insanity as psychological dimension. Once I had a weeklong liaison with an unhappily married Las Vegas mounted policewoman who wanted to break into movies. As for the young women once characterized as starlets — they all knew the joke about the Polish ingénue, the one who slept with the writer.

I was not so obtuse that I failed to observe certain patterns in my own behavior — not simply the greedy self-indulgence but all the actions that were coming to define me. At the time this seemed a misfortune because I didn't reflect on them with any satisfaction. There they were, however, beginning to seem like a summary, coming due like old bar bills. As for root causes, I couldn't have cared less. There were limits even to my self-absorption. Also I worried about getting ever deeper into drugs.

I saw Lucy every few months. Jennifer and I finally had it out around that one. She accused me of infidelity, and I told her plainly that yes, I was sleeping around. Safe sex, of course, I said, though I don't know how much that would have mattered, since Jennifer and I had not made love for months. However, I told her truthfully that I had not been to bed with Lucy for years, and not at all since we had married. I also challenged her own virtue.

"What about your supposed-to-be-faggot colleague down there at school? Fucking Boris." The high-bounding lover was called Ivan Ivanic, and I had hated him since the day Jennifer corrected my pronunciation of his name, which was I-van-ich. "He's not getting in your pants?"

She was furious, naturally. You can't use that kind of malicious language about gays to most dancers. But I saw something else in her reaction. She was shocked. She cried. I resisted the impulse to believe her.

I began to visit Lucy more frequently. One thing I went up for was dope. She had moved into a fairly respectable hotel just uphill from the Tenderloin, and by then she was scoring regularly in the Mission. After numerous misadventures, ripoffs and a near rape she had learned how to comport herself around the market. She had the added protection of being a reliable customer. Lucy was not yet penniless. Her television work was still in syndication, and her residuals from SAG continued. But she was spending her money fast.

By the time I arrived from the airport — this was still in the days of fifty-dollar flights — Lucy would have done her marketing on Dolores and picked up her exchange spike at the Haight Free Clinic. My contribution to the picnic was the coke I had bought down south. Lucy kept her small room very neat. We would embrace. Sometimes we would hold each other, as chaste as Hansel and Gretel, to show we cared. We hoped we cared. Both of us were beginning to stop caring about much.

I would snort coke and Lucy's smack. I never shot it.

Sometimes it made me sick. Often it provoked brief hilarity. I would watch her fix — the spoon, the lighter, the works, as they say — with something like reverence. Listen, I had grown up to Chet Baker, to Coltrane, to Lady Day. To me, junkies, no matter how forlorn, were holy. Of course at a certain point if you've seen one, you've seen them all, and this was as true of us as of anyone. Much of the time we looked into each other's eyes without sentiment. This was better than staring at your toe. In each other's dilating pupils we could reflect calmly on the uneasy past. The lambent moments expanded infinitely. All was resolved for a while. Once she began to dream aloud about going to Jerusalem to do research for the script that I would write, and about kicking the jones in the holy places.

We chose silence sometimes. It wasn't that we never spoke. In a certain way you might say we were weary of each other. Not bored, or fed up, or anything of that sort. Worn out after the lives we'd tried to make intersect, and conducting a joint meditation on the subject. There were times I'll admit I cried. She never did, but then she was always higher.

Every once in a while Lucy would try to persuade me to fix the way she did. We never went through with it, and I felt guilty. I was, after all, the guy who had not gone bungee jumping. Lucy never pressed it.

"If you died, I would feel like I killed Shakespeare," she said.

I was never sure whether we thought this would be good or bad.

Mortality intruded itself regularly into our afternoons because it seemed that half the people we knew were dead. I supposed that down in sunny Encinitas my Jennifer was expecting to hear that I had succumbed to the kiss. During one of my later visits — one of the last — Lucy told me about a conversation she'd had at the UC hospital emergency room. A doctor there had said to her: "You're rather old to be an addict." She laughed about it and did a self-important, falsely mellow doctorish voice repeating it.

To me, Lucy was still beautiful. I don't know how she looked to other people. She was my heroine. I did notice that lately she always wore long sleeves, to hide the abscesses that marked the tracks where her veins had been. Her eyes didn't die. Once she looked out the small clear window that looked up Nob Hill and made a declaration:

"The rest of my life is going to last about eleven minutes."

The line was hardly lyrical, but her delivery was smashing. She looked great saying it, and I saw that at long last she had located the role of her lifetime. Everything before had been provisional, but she had made this woman her own. It seemed that this was finally whom she had become, and she could do almost anything with it. Found her moment, to be inhabited completely, but of course briefly.

I went home then, the way I always had, and saved almost everything. I saw that Lucy and I, together, had at last found the true path and that this time we were walking hand in hand, the whole distance. Again I refused the jump. She was more than half a ghost by then, and it would be pretty to think her interceding spirit saved me.

One of us had to walk away and it was not going to be Lucy. She was the actor, I thought, not me.

The Archer

....

IT WAS SAID OF Duffy that he had threatened his wife and her lover with a crossbow. His own recollection of that celebrated night was scattered, but the heroic archaism of the story, featuring Duffy, his ex-wife Otis, the young novelist Prosser Spearman and Duffy's well-oiled, homemade, hair-trigger mechanical bow and arrow, kept it ever new. Each autumn it was revived, like a solar myth, for a new generation of art students.

"Never happened," Duffy would snarl when some kid worked up the nerve to confront him with the story. The brazen student was almost invariably female, often some wild-eyed, self-destructive, druggy, sexually alluring waif, a girl possessed of an original talent, deficient only in draftsmanship and sense. "Pure invention," he would insist.

But Duffy himself was not so sure. And no one wanted to let the story pass out of currency. It survived as an oral recitation rather than a text, suggestive in its passion and formality of medieval romance, the *chanson de geste*, the border ballad, irresistible to young troubadours.

One winter night, the story went, the snow lay deeply on the ground. (It was always a winter story; there was always a lot of snow. Why?) Under the blizzard's whirl Duffy sat in the cold and dark of his parked car, bitterly watching his own house, savoring with saturnine irony and rage the jolly fire at his cozy hearth. In the cheery warmth of the living room, he knew, the rat-haired potbellied writer Prosser Spearman was having his way with lithesome Otis, Duffy's wife of some years. In the dancing light and shadow, on his own wolf skins and woven rugs, she was bestowing on Prosser the turns of her perfect derriere, her small round breasts, allowing him the very wands and cups, swords and pentacles of all that was Otis.

Duffy remembered that part of the evening well enough. He remembered also the lush consolation of the expensive single-malt that fueled his tears. His sitting out there — it had all happened. And that he had a crossbow, that he had made it himself as another man, Prosser Spearman for example, might delicately fashion his own harpsichord? True as well.

Next, according to the ballad, Duffy climbed from his car with the kit-assembled crossbow armed and set. He made a grim, unsteady shape under the falling snow, moving across the icy drifts of the road and of his own lawn. There was a glass-paneled door that opened to his studio, adjoining the living room where Otis and the inventive scribbler wantonly lay. He found it open to the turn of his hand. He slipped inside. All that, Duffy realized in a combination of recall and later evidence, had taken place.

Then, they said, in the studio Duffy had taken off all his clothes. Except, they said, for his Jockey shorts — Jockey shorts and the tweed Connemara angler's hat he always wore against winter storms. Then he had charged into the snug warm parlor and aimed his polished oaken crossbow's arrow at the adulterers before his fire.

"All right, motherfuckers," he had screamed dementedly into the night, "Cupid is here."

Well, Duffy thought, maybe so. But it was his house, his crossbow, his Otis. How, he might have challenged anyone — perhaps he had — was he to know what posing, juiced-up, cut-and-paste bastard of a creative-writing creep was on his floor? He might have been defending his home and his wife's health and safety. Duffy knew better in these weak piping times than to speak of honor.

Whatever the circumstances, Otis had been very angry. So angry that she had ended by marrying the talented youth, a scandal since he was ten years her junior. The young writer had divorced his own wife, preempting her elopement with the chairwoman of a women's poetry workshop she had been attending.

Duffy was lucky enough to keep his job at the college, but he lost the faculty house that he and Otis had occupied, the very house where he had confronted his betrayers. This meant that the male tenant of the house was now his enemy and Otis's husband. This circumstance caused him a great deal of regret and rage. He had no choice, however, but to digest the venom of his spleen, since neither Otis nor the college nor the town would be complacent in the face of another of his potentially homicidal assaults.

Things improved slightly. For instance, he was able,

catching Otis in one of her wayward moods, to engineer a reconciliation of sorts. The fact was he had missed her unruly companionship, and he felt grateful and meanly satisfied to conduct a ragged liaison with her. Lying beside her on what had once been his living room floor was both exhilarating and distressing. To creep with the stealth of a burglar out of what had been his own natural space was a sordid humiliation. Sometimes he made up his mind to leave the job and the town and the proximity of Otis altogether, but necessity kept him bound. Sitting in ambush on that fateful winter night had nourished his taste for single-malts, which he went on buying and drinking for the length of time he could still afford them. Eventually he found other, less costly stimulants. In the years following his divorce from Otis, his drinking and doping increased, along with his tendency toward anger and melancholy. He occasionally encountered his rival in town and had to endure Prosser's fear and deference, a craven, insolent submission that might well be taken for sympathy. Plainly, Duffy thought, when the boards of Prosser's usurped house creaked in the night he must imagine — whatever the literal facts had been — that Duffy and his crossbow had finally come for him.

As time passed, Duffy increasingly took up the academic craft lecture circuit to escape the heart of the dark New England winter. Winter was hardest for him, the season of his sorrows, and it was especially hard when he passed what had been his own house, swathed in its warm hibernal glow. At the beginning of one winter break, with homely winter celebrations of goodwill thickening the air, Duffy drove to the airport by a route avoiding the house he had shared with Otis.

He was headed for Pahoochee State University on the Gulf of Mexico, via a change of planes in Atlanta. Years before, Duffy had looked forward to these escapes to what had been, then, almost exotic parts of the country. Lately, and on this trip in particular, he became increasingly distressed. He drank Scotch from his concealed flask in the lavatory, coming and going under the toad-eyed inspection of the chief flight attendant. Wary, he gave her no more provocation than a cheery countenance.

"Is everything all right, sir?" she asked him on his fourth trip. Hoping, he supposed, that in answer he would roll in the crumb-speckled aisle and foam at the mouth, curse God and die.

"Outstanding," Duffy told her.

As the aircraft, jammed to within a single breathing expanse of claustrophobia, swooped low over alligator-infested pastel swamp, Duffy was already thinking with loathing of the subject of his Pahoochee lecture. Contemporary American painting, more or less, and how it had got that way. What flashed through his mind unbidden was the late works, the fulsome tropical mannerism, of Joseph Stella — the poison-colored palmettos, the mercury-colored syphilitic sunsets. The interior of the plane on landing seemed so impacted with flesh that it would have required only one neurasthenic's psychic break to be transformed into a thrashing tube of terror, a panic-driven, southbound rat king of tourists headed for the offshore ooze.

By the time Duffy arrived at his hotel, a swollen country fatboy of a sun was sliding under soupy ripples into the Gulf. All along the shore, lights were coming on in the conglomeration of entertainments that had piled onto the reeking

mudflat between the interstate highway and the beach. Squat
paddlewheeled casinos were fast to what remained of piers
and fish houses — faux bateaux, they might say — in keeping
with the phony Cajun ambience where the good times rolled
and roiled. Lap-dance joints and triple-X fuckbook stores
abutted ten-story hotels jimmied into one of the four-story
barracks buildings left behind by the Navy. Layers of stuc-
coed box bungalows leaned on thin concrete walls lit by tiki
torches, enclosing tin pastel swimming pools. As far as the
point at the end of Atocha Bay, this swirl of notional construction followed the curve of the coast and the highway. It
was all as polymorphous and promiscuous as the contents of
a shopping cart, as tightly packed and equally replete with
bright plastic. There were all sorts of illuminations — be-
guiling digital billboards, flashing bulbs and bright fifties
neon. In the trailer parks people had wound strings of
Christmas lights.

Duffy leaned on the railing of his room's jerry-built balcony, risking death, defying it. This particular expedition,
he thought, had perhaps been a mistake.

To provide an exoticism to match the tiki torches, palm
trees had been planted along the noxious interstate — new
ones every year, he happened to know, to replace the ones
poisoned by fumes and salt. Their fronds hung despairingly
in nets of Spanish moss or stiffened in the slack wind. The
doomed palms with their spiky crowns reminded Duffy of a
crucifixion. Insolent posters were affixed to their suffering
trunks with cruel nails the size of industrial staples, threatening passersby with the judgment of Christ. Artificial palms
stood at intervals among the others like Judas goats at a
slaughterhouse to encourage and betray the doomed natural

ones. The tiki-torch fuel, together with road stench and beach barbecue pits, gave it all the aroma of a day-old plane crash.

It was all too much for Duffy. He considered climbing over the rail and splattering himself on the hotel marquee or at least vomiting into the parking lot. Instead he wept. There was nothing he hated so much as to be where he was among the dirty-smelling rivulets of the Gulf of Mexico.

Very shortly, as he knew, the phone would ring and they would come for him. He was dining that evening before his reading with a professor from the university. And also, it seemed, with the professor's entire overextended family, wife, children, in-laws, all visiting from Mrs. Professor's homeland, wherever that was, a land of healthy palm trees and subsisting folk. The professor had proposed to bring them all. Would it be all right? Sure, Professor, Duffy had assured him. A pleasure!

Before going out, he cut himself on the cord that secured the lock of the minibar, scattering small gouts of blood on the carpet and his television screen. He tried to ease the flow with cold water from the bathroom tap, but the tiny wound kept bleeding. He bent to drink from the faucet; the water tasted of baitfish and the Confederate dead. In desperation he wrapped a wad of toilet paper over his finger. Finally, as he knew it must, his telephone rang. He cringed. In desperation he took a sip from his liter of booze. Nothing good came of it, neither comfort nor light.

"Hi, Jim," the voice on the phone said. "Hank Rind down here. Got the folks with me."

At first Duffy could make no sense of it. But of course, Professor Rind was the man from Pahoochee State University, where he had come to lecture. He had signed his letter "Henry Rind, Head."

"Hello there," Duffy said.

"We're all here!" Rind said. "Can we come up?"

"Up?"

"Up to your room, Jim. The boys would love to see the water. They like to ride the elevator too."

Duffy was silent.

"No, really," Rind said. "They like to look out the window."

"Maybe they'd like it," Duffy said, "if I threw them out the fucking window. How many are there?"

There was no answer for a moment. Then Rind said in a merry voice, "Only two, ha ha."

Duffy was frightened by the force and vividness of his imaginings. He envisioned the professor's children, although he had never seen them. He saw himself pitching them over the balcony to descend into the hellish night, like bales of tea into Boston harbor. The image was so congenial it seized his troubled mind with a maniac's grip. He realized he had spoken inappropriately.

"Just a bad joke, Hank. A dumb gag. Trying to be funny again, you know?"

"Oh, I do, Jim. So what floor is it again?"

The place was of Moloch, Duffy thought, and deserved a rain of screaming children to incarnadine the tin pool.

"Don't move," Duffy said. "I'm not dressed. Stay where you are." He hung up and hurried to the bathroom, splashed some polluted tap water on his face and wrapped more toilet paper around his bleeding finger.

The narrow hallway outside was lined with trays of spoiling food that rested in front of many of the room doors. Duffy struggled with claustrophobia in the mirrored elevator. To accompany passengers on its funereal descent, it played them the Pahoochee State fight song.

At the lobby, the elevator doors opened with a plink on the Rinds. The professor was tall, pale and sneaky-looking. His wife, like his Otis another professor, was outrageously beautiful, silken-haired, almond-eyed, ivory-skinned. He had heard she came from an ex-Soviet autonomous zone beyond the Artaxes, where Nestorians and Yezidis worshiped Gnostic angels. Her name was Eudoxia; her smile was polite but disappointing. With the couple were Eudoxia's parents, a sharp-faced, eager old man and his lady, withered and fatigued. The two boys who enjoyed vistas were round-faced and lustrous-eyed, and Duffy thought one was making insolent faces at him.

"Say hi to our guest, guys," the children's father said. The children said nothing.

"Hello, everyone," Duffy told them.

They all went into the Petrel's Perch, which was the name of the hotel's nautically themed restaurant. The two young Rinds fought silently but viciously over chairs, each one landing masked tae kwon do strikes. The professor and his wife took seats at opposite ends of a rectangular table. Duffy eased himself in between their parents. The old pair conversed past him in French, which they seemed to be certain he would not understand. It was so.

"A pleasant trip?" the professor's wife asked Duffy. "One hopes?"

"Very nice," Duffy said, sniffing Eudoxia's sandalwood scent. Only ex-Soviets were so haughty and serene.

"Tell Mr. Duffy where you saw his work, Tanko," Rind urged his elder son.

"In Copenhagen, I think." The boy smirked. "It was hot. Like deliberately nutso," he added, glancing mischievously at his mother. Her disapproving frown half concealed delight in his insolence.

"It reminded us all of the German expressionists," Hank Rind hastened to say. "Like Otto Dix, maybe."

Duffy stared at him.

"Otto Dix?" He dutifully tried to remember the painting that had been to the Louisiana Gallery in Copenhagen. "Otto fucking Dix?"

"Sort of," Rind said uneasily. "Expressionist paratroopers attacking a woman. Blue sky, clouds. Soldiers in green cammies. Nude woman."

Antiwar period, Duffy thought. Ghastly stuff, if he said so himself.

"Of its time. Great stuff."

Duffy thanked him as courteously as he could manage.

"To leave a mark in history is good," said the senior Rind, the dignified arrogant old man.

"Damn right," Hank Rind said.

The children stopped shoving each other under their mother's gaze. Duffy ordered whiskey, and the thin waitress told them no alcohol could be ordered. Sunday in Pahoochee. Duffy was upset. Regardless, he had brought his flask from the plane. When the waitress's back was turned he took a slug from it, ignoring the Rinds. Although he was not quite aware of it, he had passed an undetectable line between inebriation and riot.

"Ah, fuck me," said Duffy the artist.

The children stared at him. The adults studied their kidney-shaped menus. The waitress, apparently a hard-living old salt, waited.

"Do you serve crystal on Sunday?" Duffy asked her. She seemed amused; it was a pretty tough town. "Sure," she said. "No alcohol, though." She turned and walked away.

"What is crystal?" the grandmother asked.

"It's what we use instead of betel nut," Duffy told her. "A related substance."

The émigré Rinds looked blank but were sensitive enough to know they had received a deeply wrong answer. Duffy, distracted, was picturing Eudoxia Rind nude and crushed by roses for her beliefs. Something about her name.

A new waitress appeared, a virtual child, wearing a little blue badge that said "Staci." Duffy noticed that the menu made much of crab. Crab salad merely, but there were happy crab caricatures with antennae and puns about crabs and claws and Claude and on and on. He began pouring whiskey from the flask into his water glass, holding them under the table. Staci came back and caught him but stayed gamely cool. Thinking somehow to reward her discretion, Duffy ordered the advertised crab salad. The Rinds ordered the soup. When the child returned she carried a tray lined with cups of thin, gruelish gumbo and a heaping serving dish full of iceberg lettuce and pale tomatoes and red-veined crab-like stuff.

"Oh, wow," Professor Rind exclaimed. "What a lot of food."

Duffy grunted and tasted his.

"Looks mighty good, though," Rind said. His in-laws only watched him. One of the kids sounded a raspberry.

Duffy sipped his whiskey and looked down at the stuff on his plate. "This isn't crab," he said softly.

"Oh, sure it is," said Professor Rind.

"The fuck it is." He looked around for Staci. The place was fairly crowded. When he had spotted her, he motioned with a crook of his finger.

"This isn't crab."

Staci's neck was very long, the painterly Duffy saw. A duckling, though not a dreadfully ugly one. Something of a ducky, in fact. But confused.

"Oh, sir," she said, inspecting his plate. "Yessir, it's all crab." Staci smiled cautiously. "Like real fresh."

"It may be real fresh," Duffy said. "It may be fucking alive. But by Christ it ain't crab."

"Oh," Staci said.

"Let me tell you what it is, sweet thing." He had risen to his feet and raised his voice. Among the Rinds, only Hank looked at him. People at the adjoining tables looked also.

"It's some rotten thing out of a tube. Made by people who hate us and think we're stupid."

He looked around and gave the room a hateful glare.

"Because we are stupid! They've invented this red crap, oozes out when they squirt it. So it's red, see. Because Americans are moronic cupcakes who could be induced to eat their own shoelaces. So this shit makes it."

Mrs. Rind rose majestically, nudged her plate aside and spoke an order in Indo-European to her children. The three marched away and Duffy looked sadly after them. His favorite Rind had bailed. He turned his disappointment on poor Staci.

"Especially on Sunday in Pahoochee. Where I'm sure it's a favorite."

Staci's nestling's neck reddened. The older Mrs. Rind stood and hurried the way her daughter had gone. Hank Rind and his father-in-law kept their chairs.

"You go in there, pumpkin," Duffy told the girl, "and you tell the thief that employs you that he's a liar. Tell him that if he keeps on selling painted fish guts, I'm going to put him in jail." The young waitress started to flee, but Duffy called her up short. "And you're going up with him, Staci, Magnolia, whatever you call yourself professionally. Unless you stand up in court and rat him out. I mean only to frighten the child," Duffy explained to the other people in the restaurant. "She's not the one to blame."

There was a disturbance in the kitchen. Shrieks and incredulous roars emerged from it. No one in the dining room was eating. Security men in blazers had gathered at the door leading to the hotel lobby, awaiting orders. Shortly, from the kitchen came a fat perspiring man. He wore a black-brimmed sea captain's hat with red stains on the white part. There was a blue-and-white sailor-style neckerchief around his rubbery neck. Duffy thought he looked like neither a chef nor a mariner. He looked at Duffy, shaking with fury. Duffy stood his ground.

"Were you off somewhere?" he asked the cook, looking with contempt at the man's attire. "Was your riverboat about to catch the evening tide? Keeping steam up, right? Then, when the health department shows up, you disappear into the bayous. Mammal on the menu, folks!" Duffy shouted at the top of his voice. "Chef Boyardee here is a-gonna skin us some muskrats. When he runs out of fish-flavored tooth-paste and red dye."

"You damned drunk," the enraged man screamed. "What the hell are you calling me?"

Duffy's rage increased.

"I'm a-saying you a warlocky witch, motherfucker. Bad man wizard. I'm a-saying you bad food poison man. I'm a-saying they gonna send you back to the swamp to be drowned in shit."

Duffy managed to sidestep the fat man's expertly executed kick, intended to painfully disable him. Two waiters caught their boss and only with great difficulty held him back. The small waitress looked on in tears.

"You no-good bastard," the cook cried, indicating Staci. "You bastard, you made her cry!" Altogether beside himself, he paused for breath.

Duffy drew himself up to his full height, which was about five foot nine.

"That's because her time to weep has come," he said viciously. He pointed his finger in the cook's face. "Yes, M'sieu Escoffier." Duffy turned to look over his shoulder, feeling, incorrectly, that a wave of support was gathering behind him. "The time has come when we must all weep. Because, goddamn you, you filthy poisoned rat, whatever you've done in there to that poor young girl — a child half your age, you scum — there shall be no more of it, I promise you." Blind to the chaos around him, Duffy carried on upbraiding the chef as a security man, aided by volunteers from among the male customers, wrestled him toward the door. At this point, in custody, he broke down and wept himself. "Christ's blood! Crab? Don't make me laugh. The only crabs you people got is in your pubic hair!"

It was all he remembered of the evening. Next day, the Rind boys found their way back to the Petrel's Perch in hopes of seeing more of Duffy.

Of course he had missed the lecture. At Pahoochee State College — or University, as it had been lately designated — colleagues rallied round Hank Rind to console and embrace him. Secretly, though, ill-wishers chortled and claimed never to have had any regard for him or for Duffy or his work.

Enormity descended. He was awakened by a policeman — in his experience always a bad sign. An African proverb he had learned in the Peace Corps went something like, "The morning policeman shoots the mice to frighten the monkeys." The maddened policeman, morning's minion. Despite the early hour, a man who said he was the manager of the hotel appeared, another who claimed to be an assistant district attorney, and several of the hotel's security stooges. One of the stooges was charging Duffy with assault, the felony compounded by his brandishing of a ballpoint pen. Brought before the town justice, Duffy had no choice but to call his estranged wife for bail.

When his turn at the phone came, he called collect, in violation of the instructions on the sign over the phone. To his relief it was Otis herself who answered. Otis who must know that it was him she really loved. Otis, descendant of an insane signer of the Declaration of Independence. But when he recounted his story, she was bad Otis.

"I'm so sorry," Otis said weepily. A false voice, Duffy

knew. "My purse was stolen in the supermarket. I've canceled all my credit cards. Each and every one."

"You gotta be shitting me," Duffy suggested.

"Alas not."

"Well, how about a check?"

"My checkbook is with it, Jim. I've stopped all payments."

Duffy swore so foully that even his fellow inmates at the county jail were dismayed.

"Honestly," said Otis, "I am sorry, darl. But I'm not sure I can cover what you need. Frankly, you've been in the drunk tank before. All things pass, big guy."

"This is no drunk tank," Duffy pleaded. It was, finally, a lie. "Do you know where I am?"

"Yes, I think so. How funny! Because I was just reading about the state prison there. The book is called *Worse Than Slavery*."

Duffy paused to gain control of himself.

"Otis, sweetheart, I need your help badly."

"I know, my dear. My help isn't what it was."

"Please, baby." Duffy's fellow inmates, a generally semi-violent lot of drunks and panhandlers, laughed openly. It was impossible to converse discreetly. "What about your boy toy there? He's got bread."

"Bread? Aren't you quaint. Do you mean Prosser? Yes, he has 'bread,' I suppose. His latest novel is pretty successful for a literary book."

"Isn't that nice?" Duffy said. "So get three grand off him. I'm good for it."

"I'm surprised at your lack of — what shall I call it? — pride?"

"You tell that illiterate pinhead he better cough it up. Otherwise his ladylove's rightful spouse will — in the fullness of time — go up there and make him eat a hardcover copy of his successful literary book."

"He's not afraid of you, Jim."

"Really? Then he's made real progress in fear management. How's his ex, by the by? Still cochair of Lesbian Gardening?"

Otis tittered wickedly. Once, to hear Otis titter was to possess her.

"You may not be ashamed to ask for Prosser's help, Jim. To tell you the truth, I'm ashamed to ask on your behalf."

"Oh, bullshit, Otis. Stop fucking around! Is he there?"

"I'll ask him to call you, dear," she said delicately.

Duffy stopped to consider his options. It would not do to have her hang up. All at once it occurred to him that Otis, in her abysmal deviousness, was helping him out after a fashion. Only by knowing her as well as he did could he realize that she was distantly suggesting a strategy: that he lean on the husband himself, man to man, as it were. As to whether she had really lost her bag? Unknowable.

When the call came, it was Prosser phoning from his office. As if, Duffy thought, he felt he would be safer there.

"Hey, Prosser! Oho, man!"

The response was a charged silence.

"Hey, how's everything, Pross? How's the wife?"

Prosser did not ask which.

"Ah," he replied without much inflection. "How are you, Jim?"

"Prosser?"

More anxious silence. Good, thought Duffy.

"Prosser, I'm where the prisoners rest together. They hear not the voice of their oppressor."

"Really?" the novelist asked uneasily. "Where's that?"

"It is hell," Duffy said. "Your old friend is in hell." He was moved to pity at his own condition. "Honest, can you help me?"

"I don't know, Jim. How?"

"Listen, can I tell you something? May I presume? I know our relationship is awkward."

A sniff of distaste. "Yeah, sure."

"The thing is, Pross, I thought I had found Jesus Christ. He was my personal savior. Honestly! I know you'll scoff."

Prosser did not scoff. He seemed to be listening quietly.

"But the individual I mistook for Jesus Christ was not. He wasn't Jesus at all. Can you guess who he was? Can you, Prosser?"

"No," said Spearman. After a moment he asked, "Who?"

Duffy looked over his shoulder to see whether the duty deputy might be eavesdropping on his plaints. But the man was occupied with the color ads for phone sex in his copy of *Penthouse*.

"He was Satan!" Duffy cleared his throat for resonance. "Yes. The Prince of Darkness himself. Horrible," Duffy moaned spookily. "Satan," he whispered thickly. He tried not to overdo it. But Prosser had a craven's imagination.

"Jim, you ought to seek . . . You know."

"Seek! Seek! Their name is legion, Spearman. They are many!"

"You probably need help," Prosser said.

"Oh, shit, man," Duffy said. "I do."

"Medication." Prosser suggested.

"Poisoners!" Duffy told him in a breathy stage whisper. "Listen, Prosser, I'm beside myself with terror. Satanic voices are telling me I require closure."

"Closure?"

Duffy did what he could to make the word sound truly terminal.

"A dreadful closure, Prosser. They say if I can leave here today I can get into treatment." He looked around to make sure no one was watching too closely. "But if I can't, Satan says I must seek closure where the most wrong was done. He says I must" — Duffy inhaled to aspirate his words most portentously — "return to my long home. For closure."

"Why?" Prosser croaked.

"They won't tell me until I get there. I hear insect laughter. I'm so afraid."

"If you tell me where you are," Prosser said, "maybe I can call someone."

Oh, tricky, thought Duffy, but he would have to know.

"Here's the deal," Duffy said, trying to fend off madness while pretending it. "They'll let me out if I agree to go into therapy."

"Therapy where?" Spearman asked in a small voice. He was afraid, Duffy knew, that it might take place at the same establishment in western New England where he had been purged of drink before. It was not far from the house Prosser shared with Otis. Whether Prosser liked it or not, it was where he was likely to end up.

"I think it's Alaska," Duffy told him. "They'll release me in care of my mother."

"Your mother?"

"Her estate," Duffy hastened to add. "It's absurdly complicated. I'll need some money to get there too, Prosser. Congratulations on your new book, by the way."

A short time later Duffy heard the police dispatcher taking down the numbers and expiration date of Prosser's credit card.

"Bacon tells us," he said to the deputy as he packed his soiled belongings to leave, "the coward is loyal only to fear."

"I need you to shut up," the young deputy said.

The locals were vindictive, especially the hotel people. For three days Duffy was forbidden to leave town, and he was threatened with deformed bounty hunters if he did so. The first day he was homeless, which, in Pahoochee, was itself illegal. His overnight bag contained a single change of clothes, and the venal bubbas who ruled the town owned all the hotels, all the soap and all the potable water. Earning a little more of Otis's mocking solicitude, he was finally able to buy two nights in advance at a washboard-sided welfare motel on a fetid canal a few blocks from the Gulf. The university, for its own reasons he presumed, fixed things with the city. The motel chain hand-delivered some letters to him and to his lawyer in Boston threatening action for damages, though nothing came of it in the end. They also produced a form requiring his signature on which he agreed never again to seek hospitality at their establishments.

While the paperwork and money changed hands, the law required Duffy to remain in Pahoochee to await the disposition of his case. Duffy spent his first hours in the Spray Mo-

tel avoiding the public spaces where crack was sold. His solitary window opened on an alley — that is, it failed to open
on the alley. An ancient air conditioner aspirated its pro-
longed death rattle. Mounted on the spastic springs of his
sofa bed, he passed the time doodling on available surfaces
and trying to sort hopes and dreams from hallucinations.

By nightfall the darkness gave forth only cries of laughter,
pain and distant small-arms fire, along with the emphysemic
cooler's soldiering on. Duffy told himself that the machine
was deciding his fate, that he could keep going not a moment longer than the air conditioning, that its vital signs
were measuring his. Like the unhappy man in the Good
Book, he had prayed that eve be sudden. At night he preferred that morn be soon.

After first light he looked down the alley and saw the
Spray Motel's contingent of moms and welfare children
lined up for the school bus. They were all black except for
one bedraggled and overweight pale mom with a speed rack
of front teeth, who chattered continually to the other mothers regardless of whether they answered her or not. The
Spray was no place for any kid to have to live, Duffy thought.
But the kids were clean, carrying books, even if their mothers and grandmothers were dressed for a day on their knees
with a brush. Or for a previous night of heavy dates. The
high spirits of the children lifted his heart briefly, but he
soon found the preschool assembly as dispiriting as everything else. It was not right, he thought; another presenta-
tion of how things so often were not. And as so often then,
things made him want to have a drink. Also not to have one.
The drinking life, he thought, was lived moment by mo-

ment. He was getting too old for it, and presently he would
be too old to change.

He took what was left of Otis and Prosser's money and
bought some art supplies at the college end of the beach. He
also bought a new cell phone and a cheap wristwatch. Cell
phones and wristwatches were items that cops looked for on
the persons of sad old men in crummy beach towns. They
were signs of some right to sociopolitical existence, of access to human rights. On the other hand, if someone's gad-
getry had gone missing in the mall, for example, elderly
loser types like Duffy were one of the favored profiles the
cops hassled. To crown his respectability, Duffy treated himself to a haircut and beard trim, which rendered him more
or less identical to the male section of his demographic.

With his colors and a good-quality sketchbook Duffy
picked out a bench supported on its right flank by a Confederate cannoneer and facing the widest flat space between the
paved walkway and the rippling Gulf. There he waited for
Pahoochee's Sunday to unfold.

The first spectacle that assembled itself was a volleyball
game, played by teams of kids from the university. They
were a pretty pack, mostly fair, the girls and some of the
boys blonded up beyond nature's providing. There were also
dark-haired Hispanic youths and a few Asians and African
Americans, lending variety to the flesh tones. In the same
cause, there were plenty of tattoos, bright new ones with
particularly nice greens. Down in the water, a couple of op-
timists were trying to invoke sympathetic magic with their
surfboards. A few managed to draw enough swell out of the
insipid shore to get up and stand and surf the film of oily
water over the near sand.

There was lots to look at if you were not in a hurry, if it did not bother you that you had seen it before, if you were observer enough — well, he thought, let's say artist enough! — to look it all over one more time. In the early afternoon a passel of extremely self-conscious punks sauntered along the beach sidewalk, looking about as scared and scornful as adolescents could. They were depressing and also frightening in ways they might not have imagined. Duffy expanded his scene to bring in a grove of suffering palm trees, a memorial plinth, an abandoned sandwich sign advertising a psychic. He kept adding: part of a ruined merry-go-round, faded and stripped, between the public beach and his estranged hotel. A bag lady with a Winn-Dixie cart sat on the edge of it; some of the punks draped themselves across the rusty poles and peeling painted horses. He drew it all in, regardless of scale.

Late in the afternoon people came out of the casinos, some half drunk and cheery, more of them looking as if they had lost money they could not afford. Sniffly women complained to the men they were with and got ignored or yelled at or sometimes smacked in the mouth. Men got smacked too, and children who were trying to be somewhere else. Drivers fought at intersections.

Panhandlers turned up and three-card-monte men whom the cops would sweep away as though with a fire hose, looking so angry at the hustlers that you had to wonder if they weren't taken behind some bleachers and beaten senseless to discourage the others. Or to impress the casino owners that there was scant tolerance for competition. Around twilight, several very young hookers came out, dressed to show more skin than the damp wind made comfortable and to match the neon. Their pimps, Duffy thought, would be just out of sight, laughing in the darkness of the side streets, smoking dope, getting in and out of unlighted cars that took some of the girls away and brought others to replace them.

Actually, the evening was lovely, gathered up as it was in sea and sky. Its transcendent light resisted all the defacements organized Pahoochee could inflict on it. Duffy kept drawing as late as he could. When the beach lights and tiki torches and fluorescents came on, he colored them into the rest.

Back alone with his air conditioner in the unquiet night, Duffy put the sketchbook to the maximum brightness of his lamp and looked over what he had. A chaos, he thought, like old times. Long before, Duffy thought he had given people a few lessons in entropy, how it looked, how you got it down. He felt he badly needed a drink, but securing one was too much work. He went to sleep instead.

The next day he packed his bags and sat beside the motel's laundry lines while the children assembled to await their school bus. To pass the morning he mapped out a sketch with crayon to use for a study if he should want to repeat the work in oil. In daylight, he was well pleased. It seemed to him the piece had turned out properly strong and could be made stronger with the right colors. Over his teaching years, Duffy had developed a regrettable academic eye that led him too readily to comparisons. It was bad for his morale to see other people's earlier sensibilities in the things he did. But in ironic ways his beach scene reminded him of turn-of-the-twentieth-century studies of Coney Island. If all of Stella's good early stuff, all those wild whirling colored lights, was about the teeming overripe possibilities of the coming age, maybe his, Duffy's, was about the exhaustion of those possibilities, the disappearance of that time, the great abridgment of the popular age. The ghost of a century, a show closing down for lack of interest. But, he thought, somebody had to be around to tell that story. It was too easy to mock the tag end of it, to do a burlesque on the failure of public joy. Someone ought to show it with a degree of compassion, he thought. Someone ought to have a heart about it.

Ready, he called a taxi on the hall phone to take him to the airport, to start the long day of jammed flights and wall-to-wall junk-food stands. Pahoochee was a composition of grays at that hour, clay-colored sand, dun skies, tin ocean. An old black man drove the cab, listening to a radio on which a white preacher peddled prayer cloths.

As they passed the parking lot of the hotel from which Duffy had been ejected, he saw a young dark-haired girl with flushed fair skin getting out of a beat-up Corolla. She was wearing a Pahoochee State sweatshirt. Duffy saw that it was young Staci, the waitress who had so innocently and disastrously attempted to bring him bogus crab. He asked the driver to pull over beside the lot and rolled his window down.

"Staci?"

She turned to him, shading her eyes. Duffy told the driver to wait and got out of the cab. On an impulse, he tore the crayon study he had made of the beach from his sketchbook.

Staci, facing the declining sun, looked at him without a flicker of recognition.

"Hi," she said, and smiled.

He wrapped his drawing between two sheets paper and slipped it into a large cardboard envelope.

"I have a drawing I'd like to give you. It's of the beach."

"Oh," she said. "How come?"

"What do you mean," he asked her, "'how come'?"

"Well, like, why?"

"Okay," Duffy said. He sighed at the burden he had inflicted on himself. For all he knew, it might all end with his getting arrested again. "My name is James Duffy. I'm an artist." He had been about to add that she might easily sell it, but he simply handed it over.

"Wow," she said.

"Yes," he told her. "And I was due to lecture at your school on Tuesday. At your university. But unfortunately I was detained."

"Yeah?"

"So, because you're a student at Pahoochee — you are a student, I think?"

"Yes, sir."

"Because you missed out on the lecture, you see . . ."

She shook her head energetically, interrupting him.

"No! I wasn't gonna go. Even if I heard about it. Which like I didn't anyway. And on top of which I had to work."

Looking past her, he saw that there was a cartoon of a crab pasted over a window on the restaurant side of the hotel. He frowned, and seeing him do so, she frowned as well. But thankfully, from his point of view, she did not turn to follow his gaze.

"Because you missed out on the lecture, Staci, I'd like you to take this."

Staci took it and shook her head fetchingly in some confusion. As it had occurred to Duffy that Staci might profit by selling his drawing, another random inspiration struck him: he might ask her to pose for him in the nude someday. That, he understood, would never do. If he presented such a notion, she might even suffer a ghastly attack of recovered memory.

"Wow," she said. "Okay."

"See, I'm on my way out of town," Duffy told her. He turned and looked over his shoulder, sort of miming "out of town."

"Great!" she said.

He smiled and extended his hand. She switched her awkward grip on the envelope and shook his right hand quite heartily.

"So *adios*, Staci."

"Right," she said. "So . . . did you have a great time in Pahoochee . . . um, James?"

"Thank you, dear," Duffy said. "Yes, I did."

And, leaving, he felt much better than when he had arrived.